D0801745

CASUAL

Translated from the Russian by Antonina W. Bouis

CASUAL

OKSANA ROBSKI

REGAN

A Division of HarperCollinsPublishers

A hardcover of this book was printed in Moscow in 2005 by Rosman Publishing House.

CASUAL. Copyright © 2006 by Torgovy Dom R-PLUS. English translation copyright © 2006 by HarperCollins Publishers. All rights reserved. Printed in the United States of America. No part of this book may be used or reproduced in any manner whatsoever without written permission except in the case of brief quotations embodied in critical articles and reviews. For information, address HarperCollins Publishers Inc., 10 East 53rd Street, New York, NY 10022.

HarperCollins books may be purchased for educational, business, or sales promotional use. For information please write: Special Markets Department, HarperCollins Publishers Inc., 10 East 53rd Street, New York, NY 10022.

FIRST U.S. EDITION

Designed by Kris Tobiassen

Printed on acid-free paper
Library of Congress Cataloging-in-Publication Data has been applied for.

ISBN 13: 978-0-06-089264-7
ISBN 10: 0-06-089264-1

06 07 08 09 10 WBC/RRD 10 9 8 7 6 5 4 3 2 1

"I often feel, and ever more deeply I realize,
that fate and character are the same concept."

—NOVALIS

I would throw out all of Serge's cups and would never make jellied meat. Well, maybe I wouldn't throw them away, but I would pack them up neatly and put them in the basement.

1.

My hands were trembling as I came out of the bedroom to tell my husband what I wanted to say. Between us were nine years of marriage, an eight-year-old daughter, and the young blonde I saw him with in a restaurant a week ago.

"Let's try a separation," I said calmly, looking him in the eyes.

"Let's." He nodded indifferently.

I turned on my heel and went to bed.

Have you ever suffered the pangs of jealousy? If I were Dante, I would put that torture right after the hot frying pans. Or maybe on the same ring of Hell.

I couldn't sleep, I had no appetite. I lost weight without dieting. It's ironic, but when you lose weight that way, people say, "She looks sick."

I looked pathetic, yet I thought I was holding up well.

I tore up all his photographs.

The next day I glued them back together, spread them out on the bedroom floor and wept bitterly. I tried to picture my husband with that blonde in the most intimate positions. But I couldn't. My mind refused to do it, apparently protecting me in my unstable psychic state. That didn't stop me from trying some more. Whenever I managed the least little bit, I bore up heroically under the pain. I had tormented myself into a frazzle of nerves when the phone call came.

A dry male voice spoke my name. The voice informed me that my husband was dead—killed by five shots, two of which hit vital organs: lungs and brain. He had been attacked in the entry to our Moscow apartment. His driver was hospitalized, in critical condition. The voice expressed condolences. I replied politely, without hysterics. I hung up. The air was suddenly too heavy for me to breathe.

It felt as if the thread connecting me to the world had been snapped. I was on a tiny, untethered island, abandoned, alone.

I reached out to people with the telephone. My friend Veronika was on the other end. I told her my husband had been murdered. She didn't believe me. I repeated it. I must have been convincing. She gasped and obviously didn't know what to say. What do you say to a girlfriend who informs you in a weak voice that her husband has just been shot dead?

I hung up. She didn't call back.

I went to the window. The small swinging pane inside the big window was open. I made one more attempt to connect with the outside world: I screamed. A few seconds later, when the air in my lungs began to run out, I heard my own voice. I shut my mouth and slammed the little window shut.

I went through my closet. Serge's wife had to look like a knockout, even at the police station. I put on the pink silk trousers my husband had bought for me.

As I came out of the house, I looked around. I was afraid. I locked the car doors before starting the engine. I kept looking in the rearview mirror during the entire drive. No one seemed to be following me.

The police station was even worse than in TV crime shows. It smelled of mice. The policemen were not young, but cheerful.

I asked if my husband had died right away.

"Why are you asking?" The detective's eyes narrowed.

I couldn't tell him. It would have been stupid to explain that, after you learn that your husband is dead, it's very important to know that his death had been easy. Easy enough to keep your heart from breaking.

A third bullet had been in his wrist. I imagined him instinctively trying to cover his face, to put off death by a second.

I realized that I was a suspect. I was asked about money, cars, houses, apartments. Why we were living apart. What had happened between us. What my relationship was with the chauffeur.

What did he have to do with it?

I asked for a glass of water. I was scared.

I wanted to go outside, but they kept asking me questions. Someone at a desk behind me was typing my answers, slowly, with one finger, on a very old typewriter. Thoughts about lawyers from movies flashed through my brain: "I refuse to answer on the grounds . . ." But that would have sounded ridiculous in this scarred, dilapidated room.

"You know . . ." The cop looked like he was barely smart enough to have made it through the police academy. He probably didn't even take bribes, which couldn't be said about his shifty-looking partner. "You know, your neighbors said that the driver was very attentive to you and that you were having an affair with him."

I said nothing. He must have thought I had nothing to say. To explain that they were crazy, I needed a photograph of Serge and I'd have to tell the story of how we met, how much we loved each other, our life together, our marvelous daughter. Then they'd understand. And probably envy me. The way everyone had envied us until quite recently.

Their suspicions about the chauffeur and me would clearly be ridiculous then.

But I said nothing.

They gave me a glass of water.

Three days later I was called and asked who was picking the body up from the morgue.

I sat on the floor, arms around my knees, and wept.

It got dark, then it began to get light again.

The phone rang, but I didn't pick it up.

Conveniently, the morgue was not far from our apartment. Holding my breath, I opened the door. "My husband is here. I would like to see him."

The woman at the desk didn't even look up at me. "Not allowed."

She handed me his watch, wallet, and a photograph. Our first photo. I didn't know he carried it with him. On the back I had written: "Someday we won't regret anything. Except each other." I signed some register. I wanted to scream. Serge had carried my picture.

In the corridor I ran into a bald man in a white coat. He smelled of alcohol.

I handed him some money. "Please help me out. I really need to see my husband."

The man looked quizzical. "Brought in three days ago." No response. "Shot five times."

He took the money and nodded in the direction of the nearest door. "Go in. Number 17."

I pushed the door open.

I looked down to decrease the radius of vision. I tried not to look around, only at the numbers tied to toes. First down the left row, then the right.

I tried very hard not to remember the line of naked corpses on either side of me.

There he was. Number 17.

I had seen people in movies throw themselves weeping on the bodies of their loved ones.

I stood in a trance.

My husband, usually fastidious about his clothing—pressed shirt, polished shoes, flawless haircut—could not be in this horrible room, on that slab, with a number on his toe. But it was his body. His toe.

I ran outside and threw up in the backyard of the morgue. I stayed there, being sick until it grew dark.

Serge's friends took on the funeral arrangements. I just had to pick the restaurant for the reception and a mourning outfit. I spent the days leading up to the funeral lying on the couch, completely isolated. I didn't talk to anyone.

I could not have told anyone what I was feeling. It was relief. I was no longer suffering from jealousy. I was grateful to Serge for dying.

Of course, I was incredibly sad. I would have given everything I had for his death to have been instantaneous and for him not to have been scared or in pain.

Then came the funeral. More tears, and the tears of our daughter.

Black dress and sunglasses. The ringing of the bells at the Va-gankovskoe Cemetery. The widow's farewell. I kissed and embraced him. I whispered something to him. He smelled of his favorite cologne, which the funeral director had told me to bring along with his suit and shoes. The familiar fragrance mixed with the smell of the undertaker's makeup and something else, and I knew that I would never forget the scent of my grief.

I bade him farewell.

Someone told me later that he expected him to come alive from the way I caressed him. But they buried him.

And I went home.

The next day I called my friend Natasha and asked if I could come over. Natasha's husband had been killed three years ago. In Prague. She had waved good-bye from the second-floor window of their house in the suburbs of the Czech capital, watching Fedor get into a car with friends from work. She never saw him again. Three days later they found the body and the car. He had been shot in the back of the head. Natasha buried her husband and returned to Russia. The house in Prague was repossessed by the bank. Natasha was not upset, because everything in that house had reminded her of Fedor.

In Moscow, Fedor's older brother, born two minutes before Fedor, met her. He treated Natasha's son like his own. He became part of Natasha's life—mainly because she had nothing besides him and her son. He helped her out financially, bought her a car, put the boy in an expensive kindergarten. He played an active role in the child's upbringing—Natasha could not make a single decision without him. This began to oppress her. Sometimes she thought that it wasn't Fedor but his brother who was her husband. Even though he was married. The wife didn't like Natasha but had to put up with her. She spoke poorly of Natasha and kept figuring out how much Natasha's life cost the family.

When they offered Natasha the apartment next to theirs, sunny and roomy, she refused.

"I have no life of my own as it is," she told me. "He controls my every move. Of course, I can't make it without his money, but still . . ."

Three years after Fedor's death, Natasha met a young man. He was twenty-four, studying the travel and tourism business, and working as a bartender in a nightclub to pay for school. They moved in together.

Fedor's brother stopped giving Natasha money. "I could understand," he said, "if she found herself a normal guy. Go ahead and live with him, I would have accepted him, naturally, we could have been friends. But this! An underage kid from a strip club! I don't make money to stick it in his G-string."

Natasha got a job. She put her son in a public school. She felt alive again, in charge of her own life.

———

She answered the door in a knit robe with Mickey Mouse on the back. She hugged me and settled me in an armchair. I didn't have to say anything. She could tell the same story herself.

We had tea without noticing its taste. We talked, paying no attention to the tears, just licking them off when they rolled onto our lips.

I asked the question that had brought me there. "When will it stop?"

"Never," she replied. "But it will be easier in a few months."

"You still remember him?"

"Of course. I pick up a cup and think, 'This was Fedor's favorite cup.' I make jellied meat and think how much he liked it. Sometimes I buy a sweater or something and wonder whether he would have liked it."

I looked at Mickey Mouse on her back, the peeling paint on the walls, and swore that I would not be like that. I would not live in the past. Thinking about Serge hurt me, but it was pleasant pain. I could take it. But I would forbid myself to think about him. In three years I would be thinking about something different, something beautiful that would fill my life and make me happy. I would definitely be happy again. I would throw out all of Serge's cups and would never make jellied meat. Well, maybe I wouldn't throw them away, but I would pack them up neatly and put them in the basement.

We said good-bye long after midnight, after I had met the pleasant young man who constantly moved to some inner music and dazzled us with his brilliant smile.

I wondered

what it would be like

to make love to a man

who had been dreaming

of me for ten years.

2.

It was pleasant in the café.

The sun worked at warming my face and bare shoulders.

I lazily stirred the ice cubes in my tangerine juice and smiled vaguely at my old friend Vanechka. Everyone else called him Joe, because he was a Brit. He was also a one-woman man.

He fell in love with me about ten years ago, love at first sight, and by now I was used to his adoration, took it for granted, and I kept him in reserve, just in case. That is, for when I was in a bad mood or there was no one else who could help me.

Our relationship was platonic, but nevertheless I kept it secret from Serge when we were married. That was my only secret, if you don't count some of my purchases.

Vanechka came to Moscow rather frequently, and we always met at the same place. It used to be a fashionable spot. The kitchen was still good and the service acceptable. But people had stopped going there. Just what we needed for a secret rendezvous.

The waiters knew us.

Sometimes Vanechka and I argued. He would get hurt and disappear. Sometimes for a year or two. But then he'd call again, telling me how extraordinary I was and how he missed me, and we'd meet at our place. The waiters would recognize us and tell us what was new on the menu.

After my husband died, Vanechka and I saw each other more often. His love and attention compensated for the absence of a man in my life.

Vanechka sat opposite me and told me about his new apartment in London.

"I had all the walls painted dark brown. Very stylish. And at night, through the floor-to-ceiling windows in the living room, you can see the whole city glittering. Home sweet home." Vanechka had a slight accent in Russian, knew the language very well, and liked to show off his knowledge of colloquial phrases, like "home sweet home."

"I think that one day you will come to London. And you'll never want to go back to Moscow. I'm sure of that."

What I was thinking about was whether I should have Botox around my eyes—the poison that paralyzes the muscles and doesn't let laugh lines show. I was starting to get them.

I had read that if a person is poisoned with botulism, the lungs become paralyzed and the person suffocates while fully conscious.

I thought about death a lot now.

Not as something special, but in the same way that I thought about makeup, the weather, and my daughter.

Vanechka turned to business. I ordered another juice.

I was really thinking about Botox. I picked up my phone, got up from the table and told him I'd be right back. My cosmetician found time for me that day, between five and six. I had to hurry.

Our farewells were rushed. But I tried to make up for it with a radiant smile, knowing that many of the people who had loved me had really loved that smile.

The shots were quick and painless. But the effect did not begin for another two weeks. Too bad. I wanted to be young and beautiful instantly.

But now I had something to do: wait. I had nothing else to do.

When you're married, even if you don't do anything but lounge in front of the TV all day, there is still some meaning in it, because you're not just lying in front of the TV but waiting for evening, when your husband comes home from work. That means that you hadn't been wasting time but had spent yet another full day of married life.

In general, I don't turn on the TV set—I listen to music.

I realized that if you go to someone's house in the evening and see what's turned on, the television or the CD player, you can tell if there's a family or a single woman living there.

I went through the list of my girlfriends and saw that I was right.

There are exceptions, of course. But then it's usually a girl who's hoping to have a family. Or has stopped hoping.

I realized I was bored. Vanechka called again. We met at the restaurant.

Vanechka gazed upon me with loving eyes and hung on my every word. When you don't feel like seeing anyone at all, the only bearable companion is a love-besotted man.

We talked of this and that. I told him that I caught yet another house-keeper stealing. He advised me to complain to the domestic agency. He used another proverb: "Strike while the iron is hot."

I explained that in Russia that wouldn't help. The agency would simply send another one who would steal just like the others.

He told me that London was having an unseasonable heat wave. As usual, he invited me to come visit him. As usual, I accepted.

Vanechka began telling me Russian jokes. I didn't like this part of his standard repertoire. He didn't quite get Russian humor, so he chose poor jokes, and he often missed the point. I never laughed. He always hoped each new joke would break me up. This had been going on for several years.

I wondered what it would be like to make love to a man who had been dreaming of me for ten years.

In the meantime, Vanechka had a turbulent love life. Even during our meetings, his phone rang constantly. He often did not pick up. Vanechka was very attractive and had a charming smile. He was generous and was never too lazy to make a compliment.

Ten years ago I had almost fallen in love with him. But then I met Serge and forgot about everything else in the world.

We ordered dessert and made a date for the next day at the yacht club.

Walking me to my car, Vanechka bought flowers from a vendor. I put them in the backseat and didn't remember them until the next day when I was parking at the yacht club. I hid them in the trunk.

At the small café on the dock we met some of Vanechka's friends, Frenchmen. We ordered champagne.

Sometimes it's good to start drinking champagne in the morning. That avoids the whole issue of staying sober all day. The important thing is not to overdo it, so that the day isn't reduced to a dragged-out brunch.

We took out some boats, water skied, and grilled *shashlyk*: Georgian-style lamb and vegetables on skewers. It felt strange being with Vanechka in public and not worrying about being seen. In the company of his friends, Vanechka was much more interesting. I even regarded him with different eyes, not as if he were my personal property.

We spent a pleasant day and departed, pleased with each other.

But I like sitting in the sun with a cup of coffee and watching their graceful motion.

3.

I was called in for another interrogation.

I called my neighbor, a lawyer, and asked him to accompany me. After my first visit to the police station, I realized that it wasn't at all a place where you feel safe.

This time they didn't treat me like a suspect in Serge's murder. They showed me a computer-generated composite picture and asked me if I could identify the man.

"Look closely," the detectives said, moving the drawing of one of my husband's acquaintances closer to me. "Do you recognize him?"

"No." I shook my head without knowing why I was saying this.

"Look again. Have you ever met him anywhere?"

In a restaurant. He picked up my bag and talked about how intricate women's accessories can be. That's why I remembered him: you don't often meet men who are impressed by ladies' handbags.

I said good-bye to the lawyer and thanked him. He gave my shoulders a quick squeeze. I wondered if that was a purely professional gesture.

As I inched through the endless traffic jams, I thought about how I needed a new driver and also that I needed to find that handbag fetishist and kill him. Avenge my husband. That was the right thing to do. Why didn't I tell the police that I recognized him? I didn't want to think about that.

I angled the rearview mirror to look at myself. It had become a habit to check on my wrinkles and see if the Botox had taken effect.

Should I buy a gun? No, it was easier to hire someone. Or should I buy a gun? I'd kill that blonde from the restaurant while I was at it. And the detective who asked me why I wanted to know how Serge had died.

I wanted to become very strong, not so much to do all that as to be able to do it.

I stopped the car near a church. This had become a habit over the last month: light one candle for the repose of the dead and one for the living.

I knew whom to call.

Twenty years ago, when everything was just starting in Moscow, we all had many such friends. Rather, almost all our friends were like that. Then they became businessmen, congressmen, even actors—only Oleg remained what he had always been.

I called him every couple of years. I never left my own number. Sometimes I helped him out with money. Last time I called when my former cleaning woman stole all my fur coats and coats trimmed with fur. Her plan was simple: it was summer and she knew that I wouldn't notice until winter. By winter she had been gone for six months. I was sorry to lose my coats. Serge thought I had left them in storage and had forgotten where. So I had to turn to Oleg. But he came up with some excuse and wouldn't handle my problem.

Serge bought me two new fur coats and gradually I forgot the whole thing.

Oleg met me in a restaurant, smiling happily. I suspect that he only got to go to restaurants in that price range with me.

I had removed all my jewelry in the car. You couldn't trust these people completely.

"Well? Did the nanny steal a couple of diamonds?" Oleg was sprawled in an armchair, the waiter lighting his cigar.

I gave him a social smile and waited, with a polite grimace, for the waiter to leave us alone. I told Oleg everything I knew about Serge's death and about the handbag guy.

I didn't really believe in the success of my idea. I didn't even have a picture of him, only his name. And some information about his friends.

I offered Oleg ten thousand. He asked for fifty.

Somehow, negotiating in these circumstances seemed an insult to Serge's memory. I never asked the price of flowers I bought for his grave, either.

Oleg asked for half in advance. I remembered the morgue and my sense of helplessness then. The horrible sensation that there was nothing to be done. But now there was. I could do something for Serge.

I told him that I would bring the money the next day. Right to his house. The next morning, I drove up and called him to come down. I don't like old buildings.

It must have been the weekend. There were lots of people around, paying no attention to me.

In the playground, a pretty girl in blue jeans and a long-haired boy were on the swings. They were hugging and chattering away, stopping only to kiss. He couldn't take his eyes off her. She smiled flirtatiously and teased him.

People looked at them and envied their youth. The youngsters thought it would last forever.

I wanted to be that girl, kissing on the swings. But I couldn't be. If I were that girl, I wouldn't have Serge and Masha. My whole life would not have existed. And I wouldn't have to pay Oleg to kill the Fetishist. And if I hadn't come to pay Oleg, I wouldn't have seen that girl and wanted to be her.

Our eyes met. The girl stopped smiling. She wanted to be wearing my clothes and driving to my house, looking at the world from my car.

I would have been happy to give them a ride somewhere, pretend to be the chauffeur and listen to their happy chatter. But that would have been like trying to pretend to be a construction crane.

Oleg came out. I gave him the money and stepped on the gas.

In my rearview mirror I saw the girl. She was irritably saying something to her boyfriend. Maybe he had been staring at me?

I smiled at my reflection. The Botox smiled back mockingly.

That night I saw Vanechka again. It was his last day in Moscow before leaving for home. As usual, he was particularly tender with me on his last evening.

I felt like a queen bestowing favors. I smiled and even flirted.

We met at the old estate of Tsaritsyno. He likes to go riding there. I'm afraid of horses. But I like sitting in the sun with a cup of coffee and watching their graceful motion. Vanechka chose a piebald mare called Fly. He called her Mosquito. The mare was unresponsive and kicked her hind legs. Vanechka kept his seat well. There are people who do everything well.

At last Fly understood who was boss and obediently cantered toward the woods. A ginger cat settled cozily at my feet. For some reason, all stables have a large number of dogs, cats, and other animals.

Nearby a young woman was grooming a handsome black stallion with white socks. I thought how wonderful it would be to be that woman. Every day I would come here, open the stalls, greet the horses as if they were my best friends, treat them to a sugar cube, and at the end of the month collect my salary and go home, probably by metro. And to celebrate the paycheck I would buy a tie or more likely a shirt for my young man. Cook chicken and go to bed after watching a movie on Channel 1. (On Channel 1, I joked to myself, because the CFO is a friend of mine, and the ratings are very important to him.)

Vanechka returned twenty minutes later, stimulated, eyes glowing. I wanted to kiss him. He was sweaty and went to shower. I followed five minutes later, certain that this was the last thing he expected.

It was nothing like I had imagined. No one died of joy. Men were showering in the neighboring stalls. I don't know if anyone noticed me when I got out, drying myself quickly. I got in the car and sped off.

———

The next day Vanechka flew to England. I felt relief. I couldn't imagine how I would have behaved if we had met. I hoped that this would be forgotten while he was in London and I would be able to pretend it never happened.

I breakfasted in bed. Around three, I realized he was not going to call. He hadn't called once since he walked me to the car after the shower. I checked my phone. I called him myself. He answered on the sixth ring. I hung up.

Nothing had happened to him. He was alive and well and simply not calling me.

Why did I call? He would know it was me. I hoped he wouldn't. There must be dozens of girls calling him and hanging up. Did that mean I had become one of the dozens?

I gritted my teeth and burrowed under the covers, planning to stay there forever.

The landline rang. I rushed to the phone, planning how I would treat Vanechka. Slightly sleepy, slightly careless; I'd tell him to call back later, or tomorrow. Or I'd call him back when I had a chance.

It was my mother, calling from our summer house. She wanted to know how I was. Of course I was fine, but I missed her and my daughter Masha. They missed me, and would be back soon. She wanted me to think about Masha's school clothes. The girl had grown over the summer.

I hung up. And I looked in the mirror. The Botox had kicked in.

God, it was horrible. The wrinkles were gone. The muscles had atrophied. It was like a doll face. And when I smiled, I looked like a villain from a kid's play: lips stretched into a scary grimace and unmoving, glassy eyes.

I forgot all about Vanechka and dialed my cosmetologist. She told me I was the one who had requested it and that the miracle of Botox lasted three to six months. With my luck, I figured it would be six months before I could smile again.

I wept bitterly, smearing tears on my cheeks. The eyes in the mirror remained unmoving. My face looked like the face of a corpse in a shower. It didn't matter whether it was a hot or cold shower.

The summer was coming to an end.

Some people treat life as consumption. Some, as an exploit. Some see it as a cup to be drained. To the bottom. I look at life as a partner in a game.

The whole world is the playing field. Life always takes the first move. I respond and then await life's response with interest.

There are no rules, which makes it a bit scary, but I've gotten used to that. There are no winners, either.

At first I tried to keep score, but gave it up quickly. I never missed my turn. Whenever I felt like quitting, I took a time-out.

Life always has a joker in the pack. Its appearance in the most unexpected places made the game even more interesting. It was impossible to guess in what capacity the joker would appear the next time. The important thing was to live as if there were no joker.

I was playing for happiness.

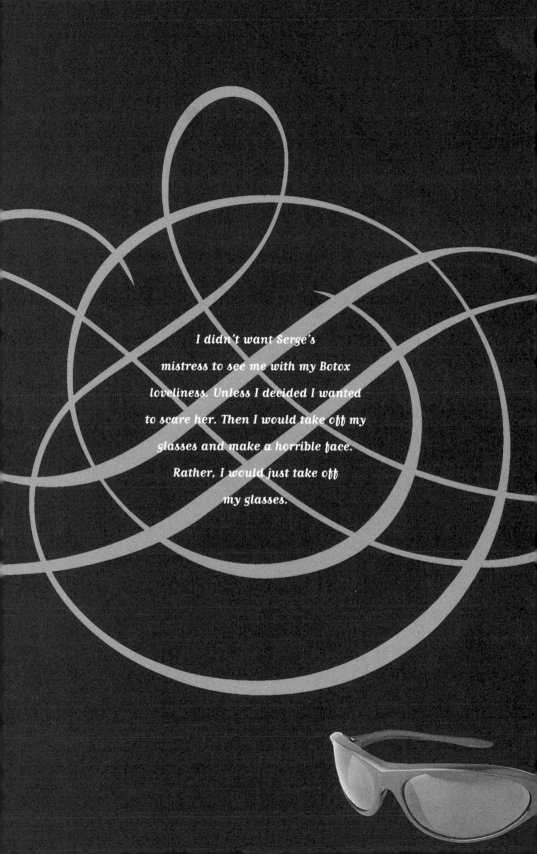

I didn't want Serge's
mistress to see me with my Botox
loveliness. Unless I decided I wanted
to scare her. Then I would take off my
glasses and make a horrible face.
Rather, I would just take off
my glasses.

4.

I should have been very surprised when the girl from the restaurant called me.

She introduced herself that way: "This is the girl you met in the restaurant. With Serge. Remember?"

Actually, I was surprised.

I was in the tub with three drops of jasmine oil in the water. I needed to take a deep breath to lower my racing heart rate, but instead I just froze for a second and then said as casually as I could: "When?"

"Why, I mean . . ." The girl was nonplussed. "A week before . . . Serge . . . Serge passed away. At Pinocchio on Kutuzovsky."

"Ah!" I sounded delighted. She must have thought that I was afraid she was the girl from The Hong Kong on Tverskaya Street, or something.

"I have to see you." She was on the verge of tears.

"What for?" I asked very seriously.

At that moment I hated all women like her. I suspected that since she had existed in Serge's life, there must have been others.

"I can't tell you over the phone."

I should have hung up. But I doubt there's a woman in the world who would refuse to meet her husband's mistress.

I rolled up into a ball on the bed. The pillows and his clothes still smelled like Serge. I had never noticed it before, when he was alive. But now I could smell it very clearly.

The girl's name was Svetlana and we would meet in an hour at Pinocchio on Kutuzovsky.

She drove up in an old VW. If they had been together a long time, she surely would have been driving a Mercedes like mine. Or maybe a slightly less expensive model.

I was inside, in sunglasses, even though it was dimly lit. I didn't want Serge's mistress to see me with my Botox loveliness. Unless I decided I wanted to scare her. Then I would take off my glasses and make a horrible face. Rather, I would just take off my glasses.

She wasn't dressed badly. The way my husband liked. That is, the way I taught him to like: stylish but not outlandish.

She sat down and pulled out a cigarette first thing. I did not stir and made no attempt to start the conversation.

The girl was clearly nervous and that let me be calm and feel superior. Of course, I didn't know yet what I was superior about.

The waiter came over. I ordered tangerine juice with ice. She wanted mineral water. I didn't bother with the menu, simply asked for a light salad. She said she wasn't hungry.

"They didn't let me come to the funeral," she babbled, without looking at me.

Thank God, I thought. Just the thought that she might have been there, at the cemetery, next to me, brought a new wave of hatred. But I kept a sympathetic smile on my face.

"Who didn't?" I might have even sounded angry on her behalf.

"Serge's friends. Veronika and Igor. You know them, don't you?"

Of course. My friend, Veronika. It was a good thing I was wearing sunglasses. I wondered who else knew.

"I know them, but not very well." I even sighed in regret. "You were close?"

I had developed a patronizing tone, talking to Svetlana.

"Yes." She lowered her eyes and whispered, "I'm pregnant."

I stood up and walked away. I didn't care where I was going, but I found myself near the door. Outside, I stopped and leaned against the wall. This was too much. If my patience were a balloon, it would have popped.

More than anything else, I wanted Serge to be alive. So I could slap him hard and then throw him out, throwing all his belongings after him.

No, it was good that he was dead. That meant he would never come to me and say, "Sorry, but I love someone else. We're going to have a baby." It was worth his dying so that I would never have to hear that.

Number 17 on his naked toe. He could never ever be helped by anyone anymore. "Never" is a concept that can only be understood at the morgue. Anyplace else, the use of the word is profane.

I went back inside. "Well? And are you going to have it?" I took off my glasses and stared at her.

She nodded.

I realized that I envied her. I wanted to have my Serge growing under my heart. Curly haired and blue eyed.

I called over the waiter and asked for the bill.

"I don't have any money," Svetlana said.

"I'll pay." To my shame, I said it haughtily.

"I don't have any money at all."

That threw me for a loop. "Then how do you plan to have the baby?"

"I was hoping you would help me."

"Me?"

So this is how a man feels when a woman tells him she's pregnant. Trapped. I heard the snap of the lock. No way out. Or was there?

"How far along are you?"

"Ten weeks."

"You have two weeks for an abortion. I'll make arrangements in a good hospital. I have the best doctor in Moscow."

"I can't." She looked pleadingly into my eyes. "It's my first pregnancy, and the doctor says that I can't have an abortion."

"Let my doctor take a look at you." I wasn't giving up.

She nodded her agreement. "All right. But I'm going to have this baby. I really want Serge's son. And my mother knows. She's all right with this."

I took down her phone number.

"Will you help me?" Svetlana asked as I was leaving.

I did not deign to respond.

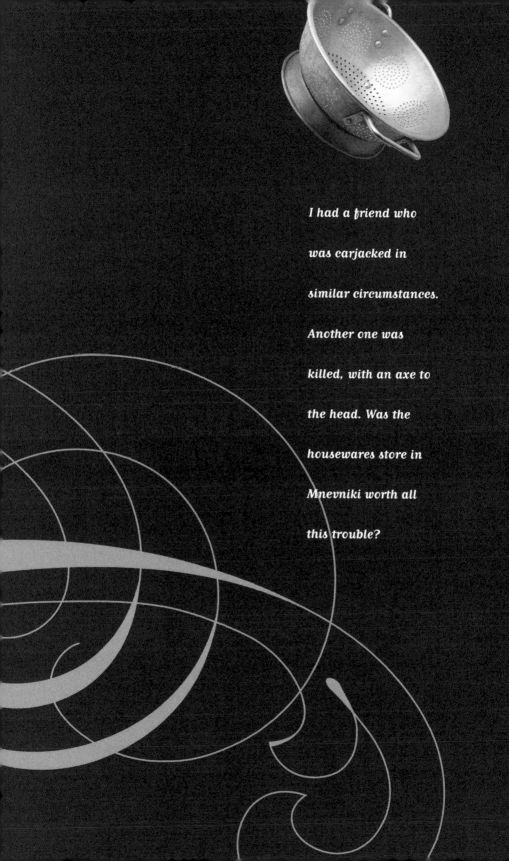

I had a friend who

was carjacked in

similar circumstances.

Another one was

killed, with an axe to

the head. Was the

housewares store in

Mnevniki worth all

this trouble?

5.

I stopped at the housewares store in Mnevniki. I was there accidentally, trying to avoid the traffic jams on Rublyovka Highway. I hadn't been in one of these Soviet-era shops in ages.

I looked around as I got out of the car. It was a dark and fairly isolated spot. There were only a few cars parked at the curb.

I liked the store. I bought multicolored clothes pins (they're very good for hanging big ornaments on Christmas trees), a round windup alarm clock, very lovely drape tiebacks, a new light fixture for Masha's room—in the shape of a big cake—and lots of other necessary trifles. It was all very cheap. It seemed at least three times less than what I usually paid. When I couldn't decide on a floor cleanser for the new maid, the women in line helped me choose. The saleswoman found me five different-colored toothbrushes for the guest bathroom. I was truly grateful. As I headed for the exit with three huge shopping bags, the sweet little old lady in a ruffled dress asked if I had a car. She said the packages were too heavy for me to carry.

My car was blocked by a cheap sedan. I couldn't pull out. Two Tadjik men were changing a tire. I put the bags on the trunk and moved a safe distance from the car. I had a friend who was carjacked in similar circumstances. Another one was killed, with an axe to the head. They took her car and $200 from her purse. She was twenty-four, and the Mercedes had been a birthday present from her husband.

The Tadjiks had been working on the tire for about five minutes. I didn't like it. There was nothing like a patrol car or a policeman to be seen. I held the car keys in my hand, ready to throw them into the bushes.

The Tadjiks kept removing and then replacing the jack and they kept adjusting the lugs. I walked over to them with the phone in my hand and said, "Get out of here, or I'm calling my bodyguards!"

They nodded, tossed the tools into the trunk, got in the car, and drove about five yards.

I put the phone to my ear and started talking loudly with my imaginary interlocutor. I described the place where I was and read out the license number of their car. I opened my car with the remote. Still talking I put the shopping bags in the backseat. The important thing was to make sure no one came up behind me.

I opened the driver's door. One of the Tadjiks headed toward me. I stepped aside, extended my arm with the palm out, and shouted: "Stop! Stop, I said!"

He stopped, I quickly got in and locked all the doors.

Was the housewares store in Mnevniki worth all this trouble? Ten times no! And what about the bunch of chrome-covered metal on wheels? As Vanechka would have said, quoting a Russian proverb, "If you're afraid of wolves, don't go in the woods."

I called Svetlana in the middle of the night. "Did Serge know you were pregnant?"

"No, I didn't get a—"

I hung up.

For Oleg, with his steel teeth, ten million dollars was as abstract a concept as ten kilos of bones for a stray dog.

6.

My masseuse lives in the basement. She has strong hands and a thieving look. It's characteristic of people used to living on tips.

I had never looked for a live-in masseuse, but a year ago, when I changed housekeepers yet again, my girlfriend recommended her.

She was from the city of Donetsk, where a masseuse's monthly salary equals the price of two California rolls at the Japanese restaurant in the Slavyanskaya Hotel, or a manicure at Wella, or a tip at the Golden Palace Casino.

Galya, who pronounced her name with a southern accent, turning the G into an H, had come to Moscow with her girlfriend to make money. She landed a job as my housekeeper. She wasn't very good at cleaning and she was a terrible cook. I hired someone else. But I got used to having a massage whenever I felt like it and I kept Galya on. Especially since her monthly salary was half what it used to cost me to go to a beauty salon for a massage.

I was driving to our house. The apathy of the last few days had prompted me to stay at the city apartment. And the house, neglected since Serge left, was not very welcoming. But the masseuse lived there. And that was a wonderful reason for going home.

The first thing I saw upon entering were piles of mops, pails, and rags everywhere. My new housekeeper felt that a house needed constant cleaning. Around ten in the evening she left everything where it was and went home, the better to get up and continue.

If I did not come home for a few days, her feelings were hurt, because there was no one to make a mess, ruining the rhythm of her life.

I went through the living room, trying not to look around, and went upstairs to my room. I poured the bath, added three drops of jasmine oil. I lit candles and turned on Pink.

I undressed before the mirror. Time to get back to the gym. I got in the tub and shut my eyes. My daughter would be back soon.

Usually during a massage, I don't talk and I don't like anyone else to chatter. But I listened to Galya today and even responded wanly. For some reason, she decided to tell me the recipes for all the salads she knew. They all had names: Mimosa, Turtle, and the most to-die-for, in her words, Taj Mahal.

I listened patiently about proportions and ingredients. I don't cook and never took an interest in recipes in my entire life. But I listened to her monotonous muttering about "two tablespoons of mayonnaise and grated carrots," and even liked it.

I wanted to share a recipe with her. I even thought of one, but it seemed too much trouble. I fell asleep as she massaged my scalp.

There was absolutely nothing to do.

I went down into the cellar and got a suitcase with infant clothes out of the storeroom. I made a neat pile of things a baby might need. The bulb had burned out in the second storeroom. I took a flashlight to check out Masha's baby carriage. It was in fine shape. There was also a car seat down there.

The housekeeper served my dinner in the dining room. She set the table nicely, with silver napkin rings and candles. I turned on some music. I had no appetite. Picking up a bottle of red wine, I headed out onto the veranda.

I loved my house. In a fine location, not far from Moscow, it was spacious and beautiful. The housekeeper had a pile of washtubs on the veranda. I had forgotten a wineglass. I looked at the plastic glasses on the veranda table and went back to the kitchen. I took a glass and asked her to take away the tubs. She pursed her lips huffily. I told her she could put them back in the morning, even though I didn't need tubs on the veranda in the morning. She cheered up a bit, but gave the wine a disapproving look.

Racking my brains for a chore for her, I told her that the jasmine oil from my bath had left stains on the tub. She hurried off, almost with a battle cry.

I awoke at six. I slouched around the house and peeked into the dressing room. There was almost nothing of Serge's: two or three jackets he had not bothered to take when he moved out, and winter footwear in boxes. I had to tell them to take it all away. Around ten I fell back asleep.

The phone woke me. Veronika was back from Spain.

"Darling, come to see me. I'm furious with myself for leaving you alone. It's so horrible. When you called, I wept the entire day! Come over quickly!

Veronika lived nearby and was a typical inhabitant of our little community. My cosmetologist says of people like her: she doesn't know how to relax. Even during a facial she has to keep her hand on the pulse. Her husband's pulse. Because if he hasn't left her for a younger mistress yet, he will. The fear of the imaginary rival pushes these women to get two degrees when they're forty and study five foreign languages and stand in line for two hours with other Parisians at the Musée d'Orsay to see the exhibition of American Impressionists.

Thanks to them our gardeners and housekeepers recognize the existence of class inequality. Our obvious intellectual superiority convinces them of it.

I drove up to their white house, bearing a Napoleon cake.

Their sixteen-year-old daughter lay on a chaise longue on the lawn, enjoying a cigarette. "Are your parents out?" I had it figured out.

"Yep." She looked into my eyes seeking understanding, and apparently finding it, took another drag. "Father's in Moscow and Mother will be right back. She ran out of something, bread or cream, whatever."

"How are you?"

"Fine." "What grade are you in now? Tenth?"

"Eleventh."

"Really grown up now."

"Yes. I used to look at eleventh graders and think: they're so big. It's really strange."

"What is? That you're in eleventh grade and still don't feel grown up?"

"Yes."

"That doesn't stop." I heard my mother's voice in mine. "You will always feel like a child. And then one day when you're thirty or fifty, you'll suddenly realize that you've been a grown-up for a long time."

She gave me a comprehending look. We sat in silence.

The automatic gates swung open and Veronika drove in.

Some Mercedes look like sharks.

Veronika rushed to embrace me, tears in her eyes. That's always nice. I sniffed a bit, too. Even Veronika's daughter shared a sob with us.

We had tea and cake. Veronika told me about Marbella. The sea was cold, there were a lot of Arabs, and the prices were high. She was going again next year. Did I want to join them? I did. Fine, that would make Igor very happy. He likes you so much, and Serge. Poor Serge.

"And how about Serge's mistress?"

Veronika went still and looked at me with frightened eyes. Just for a second. "You know her?"

"Not as well as you."

"Darling, you must understand. I was against it."

"Of course."

"Men. I couldn't let Igor meet with them without me. She would have brought a friend along for him."

"Of course."

"Don't be mad. You're much better than her. Everyone said so."

We were lying on matching couches in the living room. The air conditioning made us forget the heat.

"Did it go on a long time?"

"Six months. You really hadn't noticed anything?"

"No."

I had noticed. He had become much more attentive, bringing flowers and giving me presents more often.

"Did he love her?"

"Are you serious? He loved only you."

"He appeared with her everywhere and introduced her to everyone?"

"Well, not everyone . . . Oh, I didn't want you to know about this!"

Neither did I. But my own feet brought me to that club. I wasn't even very hungry.

"Where did they meet?"

"At the opening of our store. Remember, you didn't come?"

There was no particular reason to go. I was at the house and it seemed like too much trouble to get dressed up and drive to Moscow. The car was covered in snow. Serge had just dropped in for a half hour, and I was waiting with dinner at home.

"It's stupid to accompany your husband everywhere."

"It's necessary if you want to protect the family."

I felt guilty.

"That was a betrayal, spending time with my husband's mistress."

"Stop that. What would you have done in my place?"

"I would have called you up and told you."

"I didn't know whether you would want to know."

"How about you?"

"I don't know. I guess so. Maybe we should make a pact right now? If you see my Igor with a bimbo, tell me right away. All right?"

We agreed. Of course, this was a unilateral agreement. Veronika always got the better deal.

Igor came home. He called out to me from the entry, then came over and hugged me, holding me for several minutes. I felt very sorry for myself all of a sudden, wanting to cry again. Must have been nerves.

I would have preferred to stay at Veronika's, watch television with them, and discuss weekend plans. Be a part of their monotonous family evening and their only entertainment.

I came home. The sky was so starry that it seemed unreal. Strange, how you question beauty. But if you see something truly ugly, you never doubt its authenticity.

I fell asleep on the veranda. For the first time, I dreamed of Serge. He looked wonderful, absolutely alive, and I sensed him almost physically.

I woke up at dawn and wanted neither to sleep nor to get up. The birds were singing near my wicker couch. If I shut my eyes, I could imagine myself in the woods, in a meadow.

Why shut my eyes and pretend? I really was in the woods, fir trees all around me, and the house was drowning in greenery.

I called Galya to give me a coconut scrub. It's a good thing I have Galya—there's always something to do. After the scrub I showered and put a greenish-brownish mask on my face. It's called an instant effect mask. You have to wait twenty minutes for the instant effect and you can't talk while you're waiting. I shut my eyes and Galya started a monologue on "Why can't you buy whey in Moscow?"

In Donetsk, it's available on every corner, and people use it to make blini. And in Moscow, she can't figure out how you're supposed to make blini. And what about pigs? She couldn't understand how people could raise pigs in Moscow without whey. It's a quarter of the price of milk. You can wash your face with it, and rinse your hair.

By the time Galya was washing off the mask, I was seriously pondering why they didn't sell whey in Moscow.

Four times cheaper than milk, which meant it fit every budget. I checked with the housekeeper: would she buy it? She smiled dreamily. Yes. It keeps for a week, which meant that a family would buy four cartons a month, on average. There were approximately five million families in Moscow. I would need a good distribution network. I could talk to people who sold other groceries. I knew people.

Nowadays, when people manufactured cottage cheese, they threw out the whey. That meant there would be no major production expense, it was already there, except for advertising and packaging. That would be twenty or twenty-five percent of the selling price. Plus transportation costs.

I had to talk with one of the men. I called a few of our friends. Really, why not supply Moscow with whey?

I met Oleg at the Palace Hotel. He drank coffee, smoked a cigar, and talked nonsense. He didn't need a lot of money, he said, a million would be enough.

"Enough for what?" I asked.

"Well, for life."

"A house on the Rublyovka Highway, a Mercedes 220, a Maserati, and a JVC watch. You would buy all that and sell it right away."

"Why?"

"Because you'd be out of money, yet used to living well."

"I don't need a house on Rublyovka."

"Not yet. As soon as you have a million dollars, you'll want one."

"Then, I need two million."

I shrugged.

"Ten would be better." Oleg was catching on.

For Oleg, with his steel teeth, ten million dollars was as abstract a concept as ten kilos of bones for a stray dog.

He was talking about an old classmate. "I saw his picture in the paper. He's on the board of some nickel company. They took over the plant in the Urals, got rid of all the administration, and put in their own people."

Oleg spoke of him with admiration, the way people talk about their relatives who become successful. As if his victory somehow rubbed off on Oleg.

Oleg used to beat him up, because he couldn't stand four-eyed eggheads. But ever since he needed to replace his left eye with a glass one, he became much more tolerant of people's physical inadequacies.

"You look sad," Oleg said.

I laughed.

"And your laughter is unnatural."

I told him about the Botox. It's not every man you can tell things like that. Oleg must have realized that, but he wasn't hurt. The benefit of a twenty-year acquaintance.

"I found your Fetishist," he said, sprawling in the armchair.

I nodded. I felt a chill. The man who had killed my husband was suddenly with us. I was afraid, but I made an effort to speak. The words weren't coming.

Oleg looked around the restaurant. My behavior didn't seem to interest him.

"How do we bump him off?" Oleg looked me in the eye. He knew he was the boss in this situation and it made him feel good.

"What do you think?" Oleg gave it some thought.

"He can be dropped into wet concrete."

I glanced over at the waiter. He looked over at me.

I asked for another tangerine juice.

"We can bury him up to his neck at the cemetery, for two or three days. You can come over and look at him."

His eyes were not burning with a madman's gleam. He had a calm, businesslike tone, like Galya talking about salads. "We could give him a shot of your Botox in the solar plexus." That seemed good to me.

"Or he could be shot, of course. Then I'll give you a photo."

A photo of the dead Fetishist would go in the family album. There were still a lot of empty pages in it. Or maybe, I'd carry it around with me.

"Or there's hanging, drowning, strangling . . ." Oleg was mentally counting on his fingers.

The huge range of choices made me feel better. Somehow knowing that I was going to pick only one out of a dozen crimes made that crime seem less significant to me.

". . . throwing from a roof, carbon monoxide poisoning . . ." He was improvising by now.

I wanted to come up with something, but nothing came to me.

"Well, decide. And pick the time."

I thought. Maybe looking at the situation differently would help. That's what I do when reality doesn't suit me. A villain kills the handsome and kind prince. The princess, suffering, offers a reward for the villain's head. The vile traitor is caught. Now she must decide on the execution.

"Draw and quarter him!" I said. Oleg choked on his cigar.

"You mean chop him up?"

A wave of nausea came over me. "No." I sighed. "Just kill him."

"How?"

"So that he knows for what."

Oleg nodded. "Okay. They'll tell him."

"Does he have children?"

Oleg's eyes held a question. He thought that I had something against the kids as well. I shook my head. "Never mind. It's not important."

"When?"

"You decide. I don't want to know the exact time."

"Fine."

"How will I know it's . . . done?"

"I offered you a photo."

"No. I'll learn about it from the papers. Come up with something that will show up in the crime blotter."

"Fine."

I asked for the check. We said good-bye.

I couldn't believe what I had just done.

In our little village, it would never occur to anyone that fake diamonds existed.

7.

It was bath day. Wednesday. The best time for it.

At the beginning of the week you have to catch up on everything that accumulated over the weekend. At the end of the week you want to hang out in restaurants and go to clubs.

But on Wednesday you can get together with the girls and heat up the sauna. I have a Turkish steam bath at my house.

Veronika came. Her husband, Igor, had a cold and was home being watched by the bodyguards and the housekeeper. Veronika could relax without wondering where he was—or with whom.

Lena came. Her husband left her for his secretary two years ago. She was wearing fake diamond earrings, but in our little village, it would never occur to anyone that fake diamonds existed. Just as, for instance, in the housewares store in Mnevniki, nobody would have thought that the round piece of glass on my finger cost more money than the whole store.

Katya came. Her friend Musya, a famous party animal and homosexual, was waiting patiently for Katya to give up on finding a husband and agree to have his baby before her biological clock stopped ticking. None of his pretty, muscular lovers could give birth.

We lit candles, wrapped ourselves in bath sheets, and Galya served the tea that was reserved for Wednesdays, a special herbal mix.

No one mentioned Serge.

Katya told us about a unique old woman who could tell your fortune with her dreams. She would pray all day and get the answer to her question that night. The questions were almost always the same.

After Katya's visit, the old woman dreamed that Katya was at a beach at the ocean, feeding bread crumbs to small ocean fish. That meant pregnancy.

Katya was pleased with the old woman.

The only inconvenience was that you might run into someone you knew when you went to see the old woman. Everyone in Moscow was going to her.

I wondered what she would dream about me?

Long ago someone told me that you shouldn't go to fortunetellers unless you had nothing to lose. So I never went.

Veronika came out of the steam room and, squealing, jumped into the cold plunge pool. Galya greeted her with a big bath sheet. All wrapped up, Veronika lay down on a soft chaise. Galya put a bright-blue cleansing mask on her face.

Some women look glamorous even in a facial mask.

Lena, who had recently started dating an attractive man from BMW, was worried about his financial status.

"What would the old woman dream if you asked her how much money he had?"

"If he had ten million, she'd see two sharks." Katya lay down for a massage. "Fifty million would be three sharks."

"And five hundred million would be a jackpot," chuckled Veronika, even though you're not supposed to talk during the facial. "Imagine the old woman dreaming about a jackpot and not knowing what it is, because she's never been in a casino!"

Galya took no part in our conversation. I had strictly forbidden her to talk.

After a second session in the steam, it was my turn for a massage.

Veronika had a cup of tea while Lena and Katya splashed around in the cold water.

We've known one another for a long time, around fifteen years. We've had fights and broken up several times. For a while I was friends with Lena against Katya, and Veronika wouldn't be friends with any of us. Or did we lock her out? Once Katya broke up my friendship with Lena and Veronika, and then betrayed me herself. But she was going through a difficult period, and a year later I forgave her. Now we were all friends and cherished the time, suspecting that it would not last. I wouldn't say that we loved one another very much. But we knew more about one another than our parents and husbands put together. We knew what we could expect. We had long accepted our faults and foibles. We could be ourselves without worrying about making an impression. We were cozy with one another, the way you can be cozy in a child's playroom.

Lena was talking about a miserable date with some new admirer. She had brought Katya with her. "I told Katya, 'If I like him, I'll say: I have gum. And if I don't, I'll say: I don't have any gum.'"

They came to the café near Red Square and sat down on the plastic chairs. It was 2 PM, and her date was drunk. He ordered cognac for all of them.

"Do you have any gum?" Lena asked Katya.

"I don't know. Maybe yes, maybe no."

They drank the cognac. Then they started talking about gum again.

"I must have some in the car," Katya said. "How about you?"

"I don't have any."

"Neither do I, come to think of it."

"Would you like me to ask the waiter for some?" asked the date.

"No. No!" They shook their heads like crazy.

They started up again a few minutes later.

"Well?"

"I don't have any."

The young man asked the waiter to bring gum and ordered more cognac. He was surprised that they weren't drinking and suggested getting something to eat. He chugged down the cognac. A girl in fashionable jeans from Lagerfeld's latest collection came down the street. She came over to kiss him. They were friends.

"Maybe there is some gum," Katya said, "but it's sugar-free."

"You mean it's in tablets rather than sticks?" Lena asked.

Katya nodded without the slightest idea of what Lena meant.

The young man said good-bye to the girl and ordered more cognac. He asked where they wanted to go next. He suggested his place.

"One hundred percent sugar," Lena concluded, while their date looked at them in suspicion. "You know, I've decided we're not going to have any gum today. Let's go!"

We all laughed and Veronika asked them to bring her on the next date.

Then Katya told us about photo-rejuvenation. It's expensive, but it doesn't work. She had four sessions for $730 and then stopped.

I told them about pregnant Svetlana.

Veronika was a mother of two children and she knew Svetlana.

"Maybe we should chip in to help her?" she exclaimed enthusiastically.

I knew what that meant. First Veronika would give some money. Buy presents when the baby arrived. She would spend a lot of time thinking about what to get for his first birthday. But she wouldn't even bother to call. By the time he was two, she would sit in a bar with the girlfriends and bitterly denounce herself for being such a bad person, having completely abandoned Svetlana and the child. She would dream about buying a carload of furniture, clothes, and toys any day now and showing up on Svetlana's doorstep, her modest smile stopping the flow of gratitude. More than likely that would never happen.

"That bitch wanted to steal your husband! And now she has the nerve to look you in the eyes!" Lena was talking about Svetlana, but she meant the woman who stole her husband. "Let her starve to death, we're not going to help her!"

"Give her money for an abortion," Katya said and gave me a look.

I was the only one who knew her secret. Seven years ago, her fiancé, one of the richest men in Russia, fell in love with another. Practical Katya wept over her lover's treachery and then began thinking about how to guarantee her lifestyle. Until he announced they were separating, she had time to think of something. And we did. Katya announced she was pregnant—she even quit smoking. A few months later she began complaining of morning sickness. Even to me. By that time her tycoon's affair with another became well known. She demanded an explanation. He left slamming the door. The next day she told people she had lost the baby. And as a result, she was sterile. The tycoon broke up with the new girl very quickly. He treated Katya warmly to this day, never forgetting to transfer ten thousand dollars to her account every month.

Katya had no children. Or any long-term relationships. It's not easy finding a fiancé when you're well off.

"What do you think?" asked Veronika.

I thought that she probably had Svetlana's phone number.

"Scratch her eyes out," I replied.

"What about the baby?"

Lena beat me to an answer. "She has to prove that it's Serge's first!"

"Now, that's right," agreed Katya.

"Impossible. There's nothing for DNA analysis."

If only . . . I don't know . . . I do know. If only we could exhume him and take a lock of his hair. I thought how much I wanted to see Serge again. I missed him terribly, as if he were a living person. Sometimes I thought that he was just away on a trip and all I had to do was call to bring him home. I was so ready to call!

But I wasn't ready to see him under those circumstances.

"Girls, let's talk about something else," I asked.

And we started on thieving housekeepers. Veronika has an extra refrigerator-freezer in the basement. She bought a rabbit and put it in the downstairs freezer, having no plans for rabbit in the near future. But three days later she wanted rabbit and asked the housekeeper to make some. She and Igor got home at the same time, the table was set, and dinner was prepared: veal roasted in the oven with cheese and mayonnaise. "There is no rabbit," the housekeeper explained. Veronika, furious, went down to the cellar and saw that the housekeeper was right. About the rabbit.

"But I'm not an idiot." Veronika made it almost a question. "I put it in there myself!"

Katya said that it's too bad about the rabbit, but she was much sorrier to lose her silk scarves. She kept them neatly folded in her wardrobe, and the housekeeper was stealing them one at a time, figuring that Katya couldn't remember all of them. Katya suspected after the second one vanished and caught her red-handed with the third. She pulled her scarf out of the housekeeper's bag and demanded the others.

"I won't give them back," said the housekeeper. "You have plenty as it is." She slammed the door so hard that Katya sat for a long time, afraid that she might come back for something else.

"Do you know her address?" Lena asked. "That has to be punished. She'll go work for someone else."

"I know it."

Veronika took the initiative. "Give it to me. I'll ask Igor to send our Borisych to see her. She'll stop stealing forever."

Borisych was a former major in the Fraud Squad. Igor kept him on the payroll for when anyone had to be given a scare. For instance, if a travel agency takes your money and then doesn't do your visas, or if you buy something that is a lemon but the store won't take it back. Borisych would surround the store or travel agency with a squad of sturdy men in black masks, go inside, make all the staff lie on the floor, and instantly solve all the issues.

We talked more about all kinds of things and Veronika started heading for home. Katya and Lena were in no hurry. We went upstairs to the living room, opened a bottle of Beaujolais and chatted lazily, lying on the couches.

They went home around midnight.

Late that evening he picked up the phone himself. He must have realized that I wasn't going to give up. You can't deny the widow of a friend without a good reason.

8.

I called Svetlana and told her I could give her money only for an abortion. That was my decision.

She said that she would have the baby. It had to do with something about her love for Serge, and that she used some trick to get a job at the national savings bank, Sberbank, and now they'd have to give her paid maternity leave. She would devote herself totally to the baby.

That was her decision. It was her right to make it.

I drove out onto the Rublyovo-Uspenskoe Highway. A long line of cars was at a standstill. Automatically I went into the opposite lane to pass the long backup. At the highway patrol checkpoint in Razdory, uniformed men rushed out at me, blowing their whistles, waving their batons, and gesturing for me to pull over. I looked around and realized that this wasn't an ordinary traffic jam. A government car was expected and everyone had been pulled over to make way. The president (and the former president) and several high government officials lived in our little area, and this two-lane highway was the only road to town and to the Kremlin. I pulled in at the head of the line and started digging out my documents. The policemen stood at attention as the presidential motorcade rushed by. A minute later, traffic was moving again. An angry policeman came over to my car.

"Papers!"

I handed them to him and he took them into his station without a word.

Driving in the opposite lane, not obeying police instructions, creating a dangerous situation—I was sure I'd lose my license.

I went into their little hut and started shouting: "Where are my documents? How long am I supposed to wait?"

The cops looked at me in surprise and said something about the president.

"I'm in a hurry!" I screamed. "What, you don't have anybody else to talk to?"

One of them asked me to leave and started copying out the data from my inspection certificate. He announced he was suspending my license.

"Just hurry it up!" I said. "Take what you want! But that will be the last license you ever suspend here!"

I turned toward the door, now worrying that I had overdone it.

The cop angrily tossed my documents to the edge of his desk.

"There, I could tell you were regular guys." I said good-bye and left.

I felt their hatred with my back. They hated everyone who lived here. But they couldn't risk their jobs. They didn't know who I was—I could have been Yeltsin's granddaughter. Everybody in our little village is someone's wife and someone's granddaughter.

I had had a business meeting about whey. I found a dairy in the town of Lubertsy willing to sell it to me. The price was twenty-five kopeks per liter. With packaging, they offered it at three rubles a pack, but that was too expensive for me. To be worthwhile, my costs had to be no more than two rubles, plus delivery. Whey could be bought unpacked, in trucks that held a little over three tons. A truck with a partition in the middle. I pictured it like the one in the movie *Gentlemen of Fortune*, which they used to escape from the camp.

I was on my way to the advertising agency. We had to plan the promotion, and create a brand concept and an advertising campaign.

Three of us—Irma, the creative director, Lada, the commercial director, and I—sat around and brainstormed. Irma presented this idea: "Wife sees husband off on a business trip abroad. Asks him to bring back miracle face cream and shampoo. He returns. Sheremetyevo Airport. Car and driver. He calls his wife, 'Darling, I'm home.' She asks him to pick up some whey for blini on his way home. Supermarket. Husband sees his driver coming out with a whole crate of whey. The driver gets into the car and says, 'It was so cheap, I got myself some, too. I love blini.'

"Next scene: Doorbell. Wife happily greets husband. And where are the cream and shampoo? He forgot. He's only got whey. He offers her a package. 'Darling, all the women abroad use this.'

"Cut to next scene. They're at the table, with a steaming stack of blini. Her face is smooth, her hair silky. She says. 'Darling, whey is the best present you could give me.' "

Lada added: "And the slogan comes up: 'The wolves are sated and the sheep are safe.' "

"Not bad, but it won't fit in a thirty-second ad, much less a fifteen-second one. And there's not enough of the product on screen. It should be on camera half the time, at least. And let's have a more professional name for the product. Grannies call it whey, we're selling buttermilk."

Irma smoothly went on. "Fine. The screen is split vertically. On the left, an exhausted housewife, on the right an advanced newlywed. Voice-over: 'Both Tatyana and Yulya decided to make blini for their husbands. Tatyana took milk and left it out overnight to sour. Yulya bought buttermilk at her corner store.' We see sleepy Tatyana in an old housecoat taking milk out of the fridge and putting it on the windowsill. On the right, Yulya's dancing in a disco. Voice-over: 'By two, the ladies are ready to make blini.' On the left, Tatyana sniffing the milk, worried. On the right: Yulya's got the buttermilk and is watching TV with her feet up on the table. Voice-over: 'But what is this? Tatyana and Yulya's husbands have invited them to eat out!' Picture: Tatyana looking at the price of the wasted milk: twenty rubles. Yulya at the price of buttermilk: five rubles. Tatyana sighs. Yulya smears the buttermilk on her face and rinses her hair with it. Montage. So-so looking Tatyana and glamorous Yulya meet at the building door. Tatyana says: 'Is that a new outfit?' Yulya replies: 'New is something old that is long forgotten.' And winks at the viewer. Close-up of the buttermilk."

"Not bad," I agreed.

"And low budget," Lada added. "No location shots, all studio work. One camera, some computer graphics."

"What about the label?" I asked.

Irma had all the answers. "Something that stands out from the usual. But in a way that the buyer believes it's authentic. No flying cows. Maybe just an appetizing stack of blini. And a charming old lady. Or a child. And in big letters: BUTTERMILK."

"And the name?"

"Something like 'tasty.' Or 'fattening.' Just joking. Have to think about the name."

"How about 'Morning'?" I suggested.

"Maybe," said Irma.

"Or 'Grandmother's Blini.' "

"Too long. But associative."

"I think it's not bad at all. If you come up with something short but with the same sense, it will be a hit."

"There's always 'Granny's Blini,' " joked Lada.

We set another meeting for a few days later.

Vanechka called. He asked how I was and said that he had wanted to call earlier, but something held him back. He added sincerely that he had missed me.

I replied that I was busy: helping birth the neighbor's cow. I would call him back.

I hung up, sorry that I had not prepared for this call and come up with a wittier reply.

I hadn't had such a pleasant morning in a long time. What was he thinking about me now? "The Russian soul is so mysterious," or, "Oh, those Russians!"

Everything would go smoothly today, I could tell.

I called the number every day. I always got the same response: "The patient's condition is stable." The same response for almost three months. Serge's chauffeur was in a coma. A coma is when the person has died but hope still lives.

He was hooked up to tubes and wires at the Sklifosovsky Institute, the best in the city, after the Kremlin hospital.

I hadn't seen him. I went three days after Serge died and was met by the hostility of his mother. Her son worked for us, and we had killed him. I gave her a piece of paper with my number on it, but I was sure she would throw it away the minute the door closed behind me.

I needed consolation too much then to be able to justify myself to her. And what was there to justify? I made a point of finding the department head and made sure that the chauffeur would receive my financial aid.

When the hospital voice said that the patient had been conscious for a whole day, I reacted as if someone told me that Serge was alive and coming home.

I ran down the scruffy halls of the hospital, past smelly chrome carts and skinny men in hospital pajamas, washed so often they no longer looked clean. I looked at room numbers, and I veered between wanting to weep and laugh. I felt I was running to see Serge.

His driver, back from the other world, was a bridge between us. There was a tube in his throat. The bullet had gone through his neck, damaging the air passage. I wanted to throw myself on him, and only the fear of hurting him stopped me.

"Serge is dead," I whispered softly, looking away from his face. "You look wonderful."

He seemed to be making an effort to keep his eyes open.

"You'll get better. You definitely will. Nothing will happen to you now."

Empty and disappointed, I looked around. His mother was there and she didn't even offer me a chair. Our driver, very weak, barely alive, lay before me. He couldn't say anything. Looking at him, I didn't learn or understand anything new. Perhaps I had hoped for a miracle where there could be none.

I still had not accepted the word "never."

The driver was looking at me, but he seemed simply to be staring ahead. I thought that he could have shielded Serge with his body. But that was selfishness talking.

A nurse came in and with a happy smile told the family the doctor wanted to see them. His mother gave me a suspicious look, hesitated, and then left, shutting the door carefully.

If Serge said anything before dying, he heard it, I thought.

I needed to know what Serge thought about at the last moment of his life. Was it about whose hand was pointing the gun at him? Was it about whether there was a chance to save himself? Did he think of his mother? Masha? Me? Or about that girl in the club? Or was it just fear, animal fear of death, and he didn't think of anyone at all, not me, not anyone.

I took a pen from my purse and put it in the driver's hands. "Help me. Try to write. There must be something I should know."

I took a piece of paper with instructions from the night table and held it in the palm of my hand. Glancing at the door, I held his hand with the pen.

He was very weak. Slowly, with long pauses, staring at me the whole time, letter by letter, he wrote "Rat."

I folded the paper and put it in my purse. He shut his eyes. I was afraid he had died. I touched his face. His eyelids fluttered.

A rat is someone who betrays his friends. I don't know why all drivers like to use prison slang and know all the songs.

"We'll punish him," I promised, not embarrassed by the high drama of the moment. "And you will be fine."

His mother came in. She regarded her son closely and gave me a quick glance.

"Nothing will happen to you now." I don't know if he could hear me in his sleep. His mother pushed me aside with her mighty hip. I put a pile of money on the table. She didn't even look at it.

"Call me," I said, trying to speak gently. "I want to help. You have my number, don't you? Let's find an aide to sit with him."

She said nothing but gave me an annihilating look. I sighed. "Good-bye. I'll talk to the doctor."

I'm sure she felt better after I left.

It was not difficult to arrange special treatment for my driver. But I didn't know how to make sure he was protected around the clock. I would have to call Serge's friends.

The buttermilk was doing its job. Now when I woke up I didn't continue my endless monologue about Serge. I had too many issues to solve first thing and too much information was crashing down on me.

I had set the task properly for the creative agency and they would handle it. Now I had to find a network of dealers. If I talked to Wimm-Bill-Dann, the biggest packagers of juices in Russia, they would start selling buttermilk themselves. I had to talk to a friend, who would be bound by his word.

I went through my address book trying to find the right person. Stop. Here was a friend of Serge's who was co-owner of a supermarket chain. We met at Serge's birthday party last year. I called him. The cell number was forwarded to his office. His secretary answered. She asked me politely three times for my name and took my message for him to call me back.

Now I had to wait. This might work well. I still needed packaging. The buttermilk had to be measured into liter packages. I didn't have a solution for that.

My friend didn't call back. "He would have called Serge back a hundred times by now," I thought. I dialed his number. The secretary answered again. Her politeness was encouraging. I imagined my friend standing next to her making signs that I was very nice and that he wanted to talk to me. But unfortunately he was in a meeting.

Late that evening he picked up the phone himself. He must have realized that I wasn't going to give up.

"Hi," I said and I told him who I was. His words were welcoming, but not his tone.

With men like that you have to show that you need help, but not ask for it. "I've come up with a project. I want to sell something."

"Really?" That "really" had everything except the desire to buy.

"Yes, after all, I have to do something."

"Do you need anything?" I'd like to think that if I had said "yes," he would have helped out. I mean with money.

"No. For now . . . But I have a child . . . I mean, you see . . . I've started a business. With my friends."

"Who?"

"You don't know them. And I need Vitaly for this. I mean his stores. He left Serge his telephone number at his birthday party, but how do I find him now?"

I could sense his hesitation. "I think he's abroad right now."

"I'm sure he has roaming."

You can't deny the widow of a friend without a good reason.

"He doesn't deal with the stores anymore."

"That's all right. I just need to ask him something."

"What is it that you want, actually?"

"I want to supply his stores with a product."

"That's interesting. And how are you doing in general?"

"In general? Actually, I was meaning to ask you. You didn't come to the forty-day memorial for Serge?"

"Sorry. We were away for the whole summer, and there were such hassles with tickets . . ."

I said nothing.

"Write down the number." He dictated it to me.

"Give my love to your wife. Tell her I miss her."

"Thank you."

"Bye."

I didn't feel like calling. I went to the mirror and put on mascara. Smiled: there was the Botox. I made a serious face, and then one that was slightly flirtatious.

I dialed the number.

I needed to sound businesslike, so that Vitaly could reply on equal terms and feel comfortable. Only at the end, if things were successfully concluded, would I ask how he had spent the summer, how were his children, his house?

We agreed to meet the next day, at his office, at two. Fine. And it turned out that he didn't have children.

I went to the meeting.

I've been in all kinds of offices.

Inexpensive but very stylish—those are for architects, artists, and businesswomen (not all of them).

Inexpensive but with pretension to wealth—for those who sell windows, doors, and house trimmings.

Cheap and with a broken-legged chair—haven't been in one of those in a long time.

Enormous with oak furniture—for almost all the men I know.

With a small antechamber—you go in and the office door does not open until the door behind you locks with a click. For security reasons. Those belong to tycoons.

Offices for owners of supermarket chains, judging by Vitaly, are designed by the people who have inexpensive but stylish offices. And they make them stylish and expensive.

Vitaly was ready to offer me fifty of his stores to carry buttermilk. He called in the manager in charge of dairy products.

I had only the transportation issue to solve. I studied the terms on which they handled the transport and intended to call the dairy when I got home. The dairy also had trucks, but I didn't know whether they had permits to go into central Moscow. Or whether they even needed them.

My daughter was another matter. It was natural for her that a cook prepared meals and a cleaning woman cleaned the house.

9.

My daughter arrived.

Mother brought her to my house in her used Mitsubishi, which she drove skillfully, complaining about the poor air conditioning, worn leather seats, lack of ABS brakes, lack of memory for seat settings, and lack of electric side-view mirror controls. It did have a CD player.

Mother was born in a village.

I grew up in a five-story tenement in Moscow's back streets. I used to be embarrassed to have taxis drop me off there.

But I was sure that I was meant to live in a luxury apartment, even though I had never been in one. I had read about them and seen them in movies.

My daughter was another matter. It was natural for her that a cook prepared meals and a cleaning woman cleaned the house.

Mother unloaded the trunk as she gave me advice: "Please, protect Masha's sensibilities. All this has been too much for her."

"All this" was the death of her son-in-law. I had been just a year younger than Masha when my father died in a car crash.

I thought that my mother of all people should understand me. I thought about the mystical similarity in our fates. How could I break that vicious spiral and keep this from happening in Masha's life?

There was some progress. Unlike Mother, I wasn't divorced.

"Try not to talk about it at all," Mother continued, paying no attention to Masha, "as if nothing had happened."

That was the basic principle of her life. Pretend nothing was wrong.

I had gone to the dacha to pick up Masha and Mother for Serge's funeral. I had prepared myself during the drive to stay calm. Seeing the car, Masha ran down the lane, skipping with happiness. When she saw that I was alone, she asked where her father was. I fell to my knees in front of her and wept. I held her hands and told her that Papa was dead. That this was a tragedy for us. My mother ran out of the house and quickly led Masha away. Telling her softly, "Don't cry, calm down, take your teddy bear. I'll get you an apple, there, there."

"Cry!" I wanted to shout at my daughter, with her frightened face, chewing on the apple. "Cry! Remember this day forever! Your father deserves you to remember this."

I remembered the day when my mother told me my father was dead. I remember the minute. We were walking past a parking lot. I was seven. "He's dead. He was killed in a car crash," she said, leading me by the hand.

I remember the parking lot and my confusion when I looked at Mother's face and it was completely dispassionate. A minute later she told me what we were having for dinner.

I've had a big problem with my feelings ever since. I'm not always sure that I'm reacting properly to events. Sometimes I want to laugh but I don't know if it's appropriate. And when I want to cry. . .

Since Serge's death, everything has fallen into place. I want to cry and I know for sure that I have every right.

Masha and I held on to each other and waved to my mother until her car turned the corner. She had her arm around my waist. I looked down at her and thought that it was just the two of us now.

We sat down on opposite sides of the table to talk. My daughter looked into my eyes gently and attentively. "You should have brought me home."

"Yes. But your grandmother was against it."

She was understanding but said nothing. Then: "Why was Papa killed? I thought only bad people were killed."

"You know history. All the kings were killed."

"Why, was he a king?"

"Yes," I said, "he was a king. Of royal blood, certainly."

"How is that possible?" Masha asked.

"It is. But only a few people knew. They were jealous. And they killed him to take his place."

Masha was so little and yet so grown up. Some things she understood much better than I. "So, does that mean I'm a princess?" she said after five minutes of cogitation.

"Every lie leads to a new one," my mother used to say.

"Of course you are a princess."

She nodded regally.

We talked until nighttime and fell asleep on the couch with her in my arms. Toward morning I took her to her room and dressed her in pink pajamas. Even though princesses should have nightgowns.

The next day she wanted to see her friend Nikita, Veronika's son. We invited them over, along with our neighbor Olga. Her daughter, Polina, was Masha's age.

The children played in the pool and we lay out on the chaise longues, squinting in the sun, working on the last tan of the season, and sipping mojitos. It's the perfect cocktail for Indian summer—refreshing mint, Bacardi rum, and a full glass of crushed ice and sparkling water. The people in my kitchen knew how to make them.

The children threw beach balls, squealed, and splashed. Polina brought a big jar of bubble liquid, which spilled into the pool, making the water foam.

We argued about who had the dumbest driver. So far Olga was in first place. She told us how he bought fruit. She left him a list in the evening: "Bunch of bananas, five peaches, three kiwi, two mangoes, a pineapple, and a bunch of grapes." He was supposed to buy everything early in the morning and leave it on the kitchen table for her breakfast—she was starting a fruit diet. She woke up in the morning and in a sunny mood decided to eat on the terrace. She went into the kitchen for her fruit basket and found that it had everything she asked for except the mangoes. There were two eggplants instead.

"What about the mangoes?" she asked him.

"They were out of them," he explained.

Veronika countered with a story about her driver. He comes in every morning and takes her spitz, named Cedric, for a walk, then drives the housekeeper to the market. By the time they return, Veronika is awake and has done her to-do list for the day: drive the children, go to the dry cleaners, the shoe repair, and so on. One day the housekeeper was sick. The driver took the dog for a walk. Still half asleep, Veronika gave him a grocery list and sent him to the Seventh Continent supermarket in Krylatskoe.

The list was:

> Circassian sausages—2 kilos
> Crème fraiche—one container
> Mayonnaise—two containers
> Potatoes—5 kilos
> Vanish for colored fabrics
> Fairy dishwashing liquid
> Cedric's meat (soup bones)

She gave him the list and went back to bed. An hour later, the phone rang. The driver was on the line: "I bought the sausages, cream, mayonnaise, potatoes, Vanish, Fairy, soup bones, but no Cedric's meat."

"What?" Veronika wasn't fully awake.

"I bought the sausages, cream, mayonnaise, potatoes, Vanish, Fairy, soup bones, but no Cedric's meat."

"What?" She still didn't understand.

"I bought the sausages, cream, mayonnaise, potatoes, Vanish, Fairy, soup bones, but no Cedric's meat."

"You got the soup bones?"

"Yes. But not Cedric's meat. I asked everybody—they didn't have it."

"Listen." Veronika paused, running various epithets through her mind. "Cedric is the dog you walk every morning. The soup bones are for him."

Veronika's driver won first place. Olga's driver was awarded the consolation prize.

I asked Veronika how Svetlana was doing. Veronika looked in surprise at me, sitting up in the lounge chair. "You think about her?"

"No," I replied with a shrug. "Just asking."

I slammed the door.

He didn't throw himself

under the wheels.

10.

I've noticed many times that when you put on a beautiful evening dress, apply perfect makeup, and have your hair done in the best salon in town, you're not going to have any romantic adventures. Men will look past you and only women will register the effect of all your efforts.

I had been honking my horn for two minutes, parked at the gas station, waiting for someone to come out and serve me. I couldn't leave because my tank was empty.

I held the nozzle with two fingers and somehow got it into the hole. I paid and pushed the button. They've made great strides since the last time I had to fill a gas tank. I didn't have to hold anything myself and nothing smelled.

I stepped on the gas and as I pulled out of the station, I saw a man, running and waving his arms, in the rearview mirror. It was intended for me.

I thought I had forgotten to take the nozzle out of the car. I checked. No, everything was fine.

I was about to drive off when he ran up, happy and balding. "Ooof. I was afraid I wouldn't catch you."

"What?" My tone was of a teacher demanding an explanation from a student who was late for the twenty-eighth time that month.

"I like your looks."

"It's your imagination." I tried to slam the door but he held on tight.

"Maybe, but this hasn't happened to me in a long time."

"My sympathies."

"Give me your phone number."

"Give me a good reason." I smiled arrogantly.

He was surprised. "Listen. I haven't run after girls for at least a decade. And when I did, I was absolutely certain that that was enough."

"Maybe, in some stadium . . ."

"But not in an expensive car?"

"Scared off already?"

"No! What's your name? Let's have lunch?"

"Where?"

"Do you like chocolate?"

"No." The snobbery of a wealthy woman.

"How about out of town? The Veranda at the Dacha?"

Right near my house. That was a good place for lunch.

"You had your chance. You blew it." I slammed the door.

He didn't throw himself under the wheels.

It hurts when they give up that easily.

"It's the Botox," I thought and felt better.

We were in the new little place near the house, Bazaar. From the second-floor balcony you could watch everything going on below. Cars drove up, letting out women in front of the supermarket. Solemn married couples entered the restaurant. Sixteen-year-old kids pulled up on quadricycles, those four-wheeled recreational vehicles. Old women sold pirozhki, little patties filled with meat, or cabbage, or mushrooms, telling single men that their granddaughters can do more than just bake pastries. Car trunks were open to reveal squirming, fluffy puppies—they were also for sale here, for high prices and only to reliable people. Life was bubbling away as usual, and Lena and I observed, twirling papardelle with porcini on our forks.

"Look," Lena pointed her fork, "there's Vika going into the store. You said you wanted Masha to learn how to swim, didn't you?"

A plump girl with short hair stepped through the glass doors of the supermarket.

"I did. Why?"

Lena wiped her mouth with a napkin and dialed her phone. "Hello, Vika! Was that your 624-TN that just drove past me on the road? With two black men in the front?"

Lena pouted in disappointment. She had hoped to provoke a cry of "They stole my car!" and see her rush out of the store.

"I guess it was my imagination. We're pulling up to the new place. Would you like to join us, have some tea and pasta? All right, all right, dear. We'll wait."

She hung up and explained, "My gag didn't work. She's got two people in the car, waiting for her. She'll drop them off and then come here."

"What does she have to do with Masha's swimming?"

Lena made a mysterious face and said, "You'll see."

We ordered dessert. They did a phenomenal apple strudel there. It was the season for apples, late summer. You can't eat dessert in April or May, anyway, you have to keep your figure for the season, but now it was all right.

Vika showed up. She was accompanied by a tall young man with marvelous muscles and an expensive haircut. He couldn't keep his eyes off her.

"Let me introduce you," Vika said, rather haughtily and in a singsong voice. "This is Denis."

She kissed me and Lena, and then so did Denis. He held her chair, and as she sat down she said to a passing waiter, "I don't think all of your air conditioners are turned on."

We discussed the restaurant's flaws and then looked at the menu. Vika ordered for herself and Denis. He said, "You do it better than me, anyway. It's nice to be able to have a person you can trust with everything."

He was so openly delighted with Vika and she accepted his delight so naturally, that everyone was guaranteed to envy them.

"Vika told me that you're a swimming coach?" Lena said, very politely, having waited for him to stop chewing.

"Yes. I'm a certified master of sport, international class." He said it so simply and with such pride, you'd think he was talking about oil wells.

The situation was becoming clear.

"International class?" Lena went on. "That means you were traveling abroad when we were all lucky to have a vacation in the south of the USSR?"

"No," Vika said, matching Lena's lightly veiled sarcasm. "When we were vacationing in the USSR, Denis was going to summer camp with his kindergarten class. In diapers."

Denis didn't yield to the temptation of uttering a banality, such as: "You're exaggerating, darling. I was in college by then."

Lena went on being nasty. "You're sporty in your dress, too. What brands do athletes prefer? Nike? Adidas?"

Vika gave Lena a dirty look. Denis was wearing white Brioni shorts.

"I like Adidas," Denis said, flashing his excellent white teeth. "But for this place, I prefer something a bit more classic."

Vika was pleased by her protégé's reply. She ruffled his hair with a proprietary air.

"Where did you meet?" The saccharine smile never left Lena's face.

Poor Vika, I thought. *She's going to have to take a lot of this for her relationship with him.*

Vika didn't look poor at all. She looked at Denis with great satisfaction. The way you look at suitcases you're unpacking after a trip to an exotic location. "At the health club. Denis is a trainer there."

Lena started to ask whether he trained Vika, but Vika stopped her with a steely glance. "He came up to me outside. I had my bag in one hand, my sneakers in the other, I was trying to open the car door to toss everything inside, and my phone started ringing. It was horrible. He helped me and left. But I started thinking about him."

Denis laughed. "I saw the most beautiful woman in the world in that silly situation. Things falling out of her bag, the phone ringing, and she couldn't open her car."

They were happy.

It wasn't anyone's fault that he had no money or that she was no longer young. He loved sports and athletes were not wealthy. She'd been married three times and divorced three times. She had children from the last two marriages. Her exes took care of her, and she didn't lack a thing. Except maybe a man with such loving eyes and muscular arms. A month after they met, Denis moved into Vika's house, into a cozy room in the basement, by the steam room and pool. He gave swimming lessons to her children.

They were so enamored of each other's company that Lena and I felt we were in the way. We started to leave, but Vika sincerely asked us to stay, so we ordered another bottle of wine.

I watched Lena and tried to remember whether my club fees were paid up. I had an urge to go to the health club.

Judging by the look on her face, so did Lena.

I was on the couch, flipping the TV remote every second. I wanted to see all the commercials to understand where mine should be placed. I hadn't liked anything so far. However, the women who would be making blini with my buttermilk probably liked Mexican soap operas. And the Russian soaps, too. I heard the theme music of "Name That Tune." It had high ratings, we had to advertise there. What about "Domino Principle"? I'd better ask the agency. One channel was doing the crime blotter round-up. A lot of people watched it. They would hear about murders and eat their blini.

I froze.

There was a close-up of the Fetishist on screen. Dead.

Was this happening? It was as if someone else were on the couch listening to the television announcer describe the latest outrageous killing.

"Gangland dealings," the announcer called it. The victim, thirty-two years old, a bachelor, was on the federal wanted list for murder, and also for armed robbery and embezzlement. He was killed with great inventiveness.

Nausea filled my throat, but I didn't run for the bathroom. Hypnotized, I watched the screen, afraid to miss a single word. I threw up into my cupped hands, and I wiped them on the couch throw.

I was in the shower, hot water mixing with my tears, making them less salty. Something shouted in my ears, battered against my chest, trying to get out. But I wouldn't let it out, because I knew once I did, that would be it. I could not go on living. I couldn't play with my daughter, or drink mojitos, or speed in my car, or sunbathe because knowing that you are killer takes away your right to be happy. So I was going to keep that knowledge deep deep inside me and go on living. A long and happy life.

The telephone rang. Caller ID showed Oleg's number. I picked up the phone but said nothing.

"You saw it?" he asked in a cheerful voice.

"Yes," I answered dully. It felt as if I had just learned to talk and that was my first word.

"There. All done. And as agreed, they told him."

I hung up. Then I called him back.

"Thank you," I said.

"That's too much!" Oleg said in surprise.

All done.

I couldn't sleep that night. In the morning, I got some sleeping pills.

I thought about Catherine the Great. She would hold water in her mouth, to keep from yelling.

11.

I called Svetlana. "How's it going?"

"All right, thanks. The morning sickness is over. But the doctors think there's danger of premature delivery."

I wanted to ask only one question. But didn't have the nerve. She seemed happy to hear from me and chattered nonstop. "I'm in my twenty-eighth week. The olfactory organs are developing. I'm trying to avoid places that smell bad. Silly, isn't it?"

"It's silly."

"You know, he's already sixty centimeters long. They gave me an ultrasound picture. Looks just like Serge. Sorry . . . Maybe that's unpleasant to hear."

"It's pleasant." I asked my question. "So, it's a boy?"

"Yes, for sure. The picture makes that quite clear."

"What will you call him?"

I wanted to hang up, damn it all, but I couldn't. I talked to her and hated myself for it.

"Serge. For his father. Ouch, he just kicked me. He always responds to his name."

"Do you have money?"

"I get my salary. It's not enough, of course."

"I'll bring you some cash. What's the address?"

She lived in the Babushkinskaya district. The street name meant nothing to me. I wrote down the address and hung up.

I had one more call to make. I had a debt to pay. I called Oleg's number. A week had passed since the television report.

"I can't meet with you today," he said in a very mannered tone, "or tomorrow. Maybe at the end of the week." I had the feeling he was checking his schedule in his organizer. "Look, let's do it next Monday, call me again to double-check, but I've got you penciled in for two. Is that all right?"

I was bewildered. Where had he picked that up? With my twenty-five thousand in his pocket, he must be feeling very important. Playing at tycoon. By Monday he'll have a secretary or something. Hilarious.

Finding Svetlana's house was not easy. Babushkinskaya made my old neighborhood seem like Manhattan. Some crazy old woman at an intersection hit my headlight with a wooden stick. Then she turned and waved her fist at me. I wasn't sure that my headlight had survived, but I didn't risk getting out to check. And what could I do with the old woman, anyway? Give her money was the only thing I could do. I once bought three bundles of dried herbs from an old woman outside the supermarket. She was very touching; she had tied the bouquets with ribbon and assured me that this was a special selection for pickling cucumbers. I imagined her gathering the herbs somewhere in this neighborhood, near her house, sniffing twigs and leaves and figuring out what to add to make it tastier and how much she could charge. I never make pickles, but I bought all three bouquets, at ten rubles each, without bargaining. I put them in the backseat, so she wouldn't see me throwing them away later. I pulled a short distance away and suddenly wanted to cry. I turned around and went in search of her, peering into the crowded street. She was walking along, pleased with her clever sale. I ran up to her. "Please, take this," and handed her some money. She thanked me and then watched me go, surprised and helpless.

———————

Svetlana lived on the fifth floor of a walk-up. I had the feeling that no one else lived in this crumbling building.

"Don't be silly," she said. "This is still a fine place. Look, there's water."

She demonstrated the running water in the sink. We were in the kitchen and I had the honor as guest of sitting on the sole stool. There was a table, but under ordinary circumstances I wouldn't have called it that.

To the left of the front door was a shut door that led to the bedroom and I hoped very much that I wouldn't have to go in there.

Svetlana poured tea and shook out some cookies onto a plain white plate, unencumbered by ornamentation. She was wearing denim overalls and a bright orange T-shirt. Her blonde hair was tied back into a ponytail and she looked like a pregnant kangaroo.

"Want to touch it?" she offered, bringing my hand to her belly.

"No." I smiled politely, not to seem rude.

I was certain that Serge had never been in that apartment. "Where did you meet my husband?" I asked coldly.

Svetlana was silent for a moment and then shook her head stubbornly. "Sorry," she said with great dignity. "I won't talk about that. I don't think Serge would have wanted me to. And it won't make you think better of him. You might start thinking badly of him, looking down from your ivory tower. I can't. I love him." She stopped, her hands resting on her belly in the typical pose of all pregnant women.

"What a bitch!" must have been written on my face, because she looked away. I was furious. How dare she, that little whore?

"Fine." I managed a smile. I wasn't going to make a scene here. "Excellent tea."

I thought about Catherine the Great. Whenever her courtiers infuriated her, she would hold water in her mouth, to keep from yelling at them. Often she took a sip even before the audience began. A great woman. Yet she tormented Princess Tarakanova in the Fortress of Peter and Paul. The princess had been pregnant.

"It's jasmine," Svetlana said, and showed me the package.

It was the same tea I bought at home. Expensive but with incomparable flavor.

"When are you due?"

"In three months."

I took a stack of bills, still in the bank wrapping. "Here. Get yourself an apartment, all right? You can't bring a baby back here."

I meant Serge's baby.

She practically kissed my hands. I felt uncomfortable, but good. I hurried to leave, but gave her a real smile as I went. I promised to call the following week.

Thank God, no one had damaged my car in her courtyard. I looked up, expecting to see Svetlana's belly in the window. The windows were empty. There weren't even any curtains.

Monday, I called Oleg. Strangely enough, he picked up himself. Tired of playing big shot, I figured.

We agreed to meet at two in the usual place. I was twenty minutes late, and he felt it necessary to chide me.

He had changed. If I hadn't known him all those years, I would have taken him for a successful businessman. There was something elusive in the details but very proper on the whole that created an impression of success and confidence.

I openly admired the change in Oleg. Even his teeth didn't seem to be made of steel. He must have read my mind. "Thursday I start getting them capped," he said, clicking his metal jaws. "I simply haven't had the time."

"What have you been so busy with?" I asked mockingly. "Some big wholesale order?"

"I met with my old classmate Kolya," Oleg said, ignoring my question, "and now I'm working with him."

"As what?"

"I'm not sure myself. Something between chief of security and personal assistant. Everyone needs close friends, you know?"

I did. I could have used some, too. But where you do you find them? "Is that your old friend from the newspaper?"

"Yes. What a guy. And he's surrounded by all these sharks, they all want to make money off him."

"I see."

Oleg handed me the menu. "What shall I order for you?"

I accepted the new rules. "I'd like tangerine juice. And avocado and shrimp salad."

He waved to the waiter and ordered.

"And where did you find your old pal?"

"That's a long story. First I called his office, but no one would put me through. I called five times. Then I had to organize a reunion. I found almost everyone's phone number. You know a lot of people are still friends. But most importantly, I found her number."

"Whose?" I hadn't expected Oleg to be this enterprising.

"Sonya Petrova. She was his first love. She got married right after high school. My pal suffered another five years, all through college. Anyway, I talked Sonya into calling him. They wouldn't put her through, either, but took a message. He called back in about five minutes. She asked him to help her organize it. He might not have come at all if she hadn't asked him for help. He couldn't refuse her. So the three of us were the committee and it was terrific. He rented a huge yacht. I knew he was showing off for her. I helped him but pretended not to know. He appreciated that."

"And then what?" I love a good love story. "That night on the ship, under the stars, he told her he still loved her?"

"No, he got off the ship a half hour after it started, once he had a good look at all his old schoolmates and realized what they would be like after all the whiskey and rum. I got off with him. She stayed. She was already drunk and didn't want to leave the party. Stupid. He and I had a drink in his car. And he said, 'She's stupid, or I don't understand anything at all.'"

"She's stupid," I concurred. "Is he ugly?"

"Better looking than the others!" Oleg took offense on behalf of his friend.

"All right," I said, laughing.

Oleg looked at his watch.

"Are you in a hurry?" I asked. "I had wanted to have a coffee."

"No, it's fine. I have an appointment later. He's doing charitable works. Transfers money every month. I have to check the accounts. I think it's all honest, but it's better to check . . . There was one incident . . . I took care of it. The guilty were punished."

"I don't doubt it."

I pushed the plastic-wrapped packet of money toward him. "Here. It's twenty-five."

He nodded. "If you ever need help, just call," he said.

"Thanks."

Money spoils people later, I thought. *First it makes them better. Or maybe, spoiled people don't get any more spoiled than they are.*

"Listen, who's Vova the Rat?" Oleg asked me.

"I don't know." I shrugged. "Am I supposed to?"

"No."

A strange couple came into the place. He was wearing a striped navy shirt, she was wearing diamonds. *Wonder if her husband died?* I thought.

"Lowlife," Oleg said. "Not local."

The guy ordered Blue Label whiskey. He didn't seem to be living it up on her money. We heard snatches of their conversation. Chechnya was mentioned several times.

"He must be back from the war," Oleg said. "They all come back hard-boiled."

The driver opened the door of a new Mercedes. Oleg nodded a good-bye, tossed the money into the backseat and then climbed in. The windows were tinted but I could picture him lighting a cigar and clicking the television remote. Or maybe his car didn't have a TV.

I was so tired that I got lost on the Ring Road.
I pulled over to the side and bawled
because I couldn't find my way home.

12.

The advertising campaign for Granny's Blinchiki included a thirty-second ad that would be shown twelve times a day on four channels, and five times in prime time on ORT, RTR, and DRV. As a bonus, on every channel a fifteen-second miniversion was shown twice. We had forty billboards on every main street in town. Thirty thousand stickers were printed, to be used in stores. Full-page articles were commissioned in *Kommersant Daily* and *Evening Moscow*. Granny's Blinchiki buttermilk became the official sponsor of three installments of a popular home and cooking television show. The budget for three months was one million dollars.

A contract was signed with the Razvilka chain, which would sell the buttermilk we delivered from the plant. A contract was signed with the Lubertsy Dairy to buy ten tons of buttermilk daily and another contract to rent six hundred square meters of space from them.

We bought packaging machinery, which was installed in the rented space at the dairy.

Fifty people were hired. A specialist was hired to work on increasing the shelf life of the product, which would reduce costs by thirty percent.

I mortgaged my house at twelve percent, because I didn't have that much money. I left the house early in the morning and came back when it was very, very early morning.

I was so tired that I got lost on the Ring Road, the beltway around

Moscow. I pulled over to the side and bawled because I couldn't find my way home.

All my thoughts were so filled with buttermilk that I didn't notice that I had stopped thinking about Serge. Once I spent a whole day without thinking of him. I realized it when I was laying my head down on the much-longed-for pillow. "I'll marry again. And have twins," I thought, maybe when I was already asleep.

The entire process had to be supervised. Ten tons of buttermilk had to be packaged and delivered daily. The invoices had to be written. The masses of paperwork had to be checked. Every now and then I had to go out to some police pound and pay fines to get one of our trucks back on the road. I had to deal with the loss of returns that were past their sell-by date. And the next morning, it would start all over again.

Three weeks into the project, I couldn't wake up one morning. I didn't wake up in the afternoon. I woke up only the next morning. The horror I felt was comparable only to the effects of the Botox. I grabbed the phone. The staff reported that everything was fine and that nothing had happened. That's when I set my workday from eight to six. No more than that. And weekends off. And I headed for work. It was a Thursday.

I sat on a homemade bench by Serge's grave. I looked at the point where the fir trees ended and the sky began. That was where this life ended and the other began.

I touched his lips on the photo that was part of the marble gravestone. Loneliness paralyzed me.

Never means death.

"I miss you, Serge," I whispered like a prayer.

"I miss you, Serge!" I shouted. Every grave echoed in response.

"I miss you, Serge." Everything inside me tore and burst and flew off to the place where the trees ended.

There was something else, very important, between him and me. "I avenged you," I whispered soundlessly.

We were close once again. Together again. Even after his death, our souls were holding hands.

I got into the car automatically. I wouldn't have noticed if I were sitting on a cloud or a camel.

My phone vibrated and then rang in my pocket. Veronika's number elicited no emotional response. The phone kept ringing.

"Hello." I sounded hoarse. But I couldn't hide myself from the constant lie in my emotions.

"Where are you?" Veronika asked suspiciously.

"At the cemetery. I'm just leaving."

She was silent, out of respect for something she couldn't quite formulate. Serge's memory. "I'm at home."

"Is something wrong?" I could tell from her tone.

"Yes. Igor hasn't been home for three nights now."

Again, I thought. I asked, "Has he called?"

"Yes, he spoke with the housekeeper. Some nonsense about a white attaché case. He must have been high as a kite."

"What about the attaché case?"

" 'Get my white attaché case from the boiler room and a ski sweater,' he said. 'Get them ready, I'll come pick them up.' "

"Veronika, what white attaché case?" I turned the car in the direction of Veronika's.

"How do I know? He never had a white case!"

"That's weird." And funny. "Did you at least look in the boiler room?"

"Of course, I did!" Veronika shouted. "Let him just try to show up. I'll show him the white attaché case and the ski sweater!" She sobbed, and then again, but pulled herself together. "This is horrible. That idiot!"

I drove up to her house at the same time as Nikita. The driver was bringing her son home from school.

"How's tricks?" I asked my daughter's friend.

"Fine. Let me show you what we did in art class." He reached into his school bag as he was walking. All his notebooks fell out, and as he started to gather them up, the bag holding his change of shoes fell into a puddle.

"Pick that up, hurry!" Nikita yelled at me. "I'll go distract Mother."

I picked up his things and went inside. My friend was in the entry scolding her son. He was forty-five minutes late and now he was late for his English lesson.

"I was looking for my book bag," Nikita tried to explain. "The bints hid it."

"Not bints, girls!" Veronika shouted.

"Well, girls then." He hurried to the kitchen, where the table was set for him.

"Your whole family seems to be having trouble finding briefcases today," I remarked.

"Awful!" Veronika shut her eyes dramatically. "They're monsters."

"What are you going to do?" I began a constructive dialogue.

"I don't know." She sat down and stared at her slippers.

"Will you throw him out?"

"I will. I've had it. I'm sick and tired of this. He can take everything, I don't need a thing."

I heard this story approximately every three months. For the same reason, and with the same intonations.

They've been together fifteen years. She loved him, and he knew it.

"He loves you, you know," I said.

"I don't need anything. Not love, nothing." But she started crying. "You don't know where he is at night. With whom? When will this end?"

I stroked her hair and offered one cliché after another.

"He won't let me go," Veronika sobbed. "He'll take the children. He'll take everything."

"Because he loves you. And you love him . . . How many times have you forgiven him?"

"Enough. I'm sick of it."

She wailed, not caring who heard her.

My eyes filled with tears. There was no constructive dialogue.

"And what is it with the white attaché case?" Veronika couldn't let it go. "And the ski sweater? Why? He called at 6 AM on purpose knowing that only the housekeeper would pick up . . . Maybe he's planning to go somewhere?"

"Sure he is. Skiing in the mountains. With a white attaché case. That he kept hidden in the boiler room. He was kidnapped, there was this system of black paths . . . Veronika, it's crazy!"

The telephone on the table rang. I looked at my weepy friend and she shook her head. "You handle it, please."

It was her older daughter. She asked me to tell her mother that everything was fine and that she was at Friday's. I told her.

"Just imagine," Veronika said after blowing her nose loudly. "Her Mitya, you know, her boyfriend, whose father is a congressman, he's working as a waiter at Friday's on the weekends."

"You're kidding!" I cheered up.

"And now she's hanging around there all the time, working out a plan for them."

"And where are his bodyguards?"

"I don't know," Veronika said and stopped to think. "They must be guarding Friday's."

"Why does he need to do that?" It's not every day that the children of congressmen work in places like that.

"Maybe it's a way of winning votes?"

"I don't know. If enough people learn about it, I suppose so."

"Want some tea?"

"Sure."

Veronika opened the door a crack and shouted, "Irina! Bring us some tea." She shut it again and went back to her armchair, tucking her feet under her.

"Do you want to call him?"

"No, I'm not going to do that. I called my mother. She's going to come over, just in case. I don't know what's going on with him and his attaché cases . . . Maybe, he's lost his mind . . . I have children."

"Right."

"He starts hitting, you know. As soon as I say that I'm leaving him."

"Should you get some bodyguards?"

Veronika thought about it. I pictured Igor coming home after three days' absence, sleepy, weary, and hungry, coming back to his own house to pick up his white attaché case and ski sweater from the boiler room, and instead finds all these big toughs with shaved heads and semiautomatics all over the place. He'd really think he had lost his mind.

I described the picture to Veronika.

"And he says, 'Who are they?' And I say, 'Who? What? We're all alone.' He runs up to them, tugs at their mustaches, and they say nothing. And I ask, 'Darling, what are you doing?' When he finally falls asleep, we send them all back. In the morning he thinks he was hallucinating and gives up drinking, smoking, and snorting."

"Terrific."

The housekeeper came in, bearing a wicker tray. She poured out the tea and asked if we were hungry. She had just made a baked farmer cheese casserole. We weren't.

Nikita dropped in to kiss his mother and leave for his English class. He waved to me. In the doorway, he turned. "Mama, will you buy me a printer for Christmas?"

"A printer? What for?"

"Well, I have a computer. I have everything except the printer. A color one."

"I won't. Do you know how much they cost? And you don't need it."

"All right." Nikita wasn't upset in the least. "I'll ask Santa."

We waited for the door to shut behind him and laughed.

"Papa's here!" Nikita's happy voice came from far inside the house.

"Ha, Santa in person." There was poorly disguised relief in Veronika's voice.

I left through the veranda and went home.

Wednesday, steaming in the bath and smeared with all kinds of creams and masks, we discussed Lena's affair.

He was thirty-seven, divorced, handsome, with no striking vices: didn't seem to be a drug addict, a pervert, gay, or a pedophile. He gave her flowers, wasn't impotent, and asked about her mother's health. The hookers in night clubs didn't greet him by name. He repaired Lena's car, did not drink booze in the morning, and gave her his direct cell number, without a secretary buffer. He did not use a flashy Dupont lighter, polished his shoes, did not wear the clichéd Cartier eyeglasses, and didn't flirt with saleswomen. Lena fell in love.

He was in the furniture business.

Lena visited his stores and, as a polite young lady, praised the quality and design of his wares. He offered to refurnish her house, letting her pick out whatever she wanted. Now we were deciding whether she should accept his offer, and if so, in what amount.

There were three of us: Lena, Katya, and I.

"Basically, everything I have is old," Lena began. "My husband bought it ten years ago. I'm sick of it."

"Fine then!" I thought she should take the new furniture.

"But we've only been dating a month." Lena didn't want to ruin his image of her.

"So what? Do you want me to go with you to pick things out?" Katya wanted to meet him.

"No." Lena wasn't about to risk losing him to anyone.

"So, what do you need? Living room, kitchen for sure—" I began the list.

"He doesn't sell kitchens," Lena interrupted.

"Too bad, they're the most expensive."

"His stuff is expensive enough!" Katya was being encouraging.

"All right, then." I resumed the list. "Living room, entry, your bedroom, guest room—"

"I want to do the living room in a Chinese style," Lena said with a pout.

"Go ahead. Why not Indian, if you want?" I shrugged.

Lena threw off her sheet and went into the steam room.

"Who'd like a massage?" Galya offered.

"I want a soapy one." I lay down on the massage table. Galya moved a sponge that was so soft it must have been nothing but soap bubbles all over my body. I melted in bliss and didn't notice that Veronika had come in.

She was on a chaise still dressed in jeans and sunglasses, with a cigarette in her mouth. I said nothing but regarded her in surprise. Then I burst out, "Why so mysterious?"

The glass door of the steam room opened, releasing bergamot-scented steam, and the sweat-glistening girls ran out and jumped into the cold pool.

"Don't you dare smoke!" Lena shouted between dives.

"It's health day!" Katya added, gulping air.

"Why don't you get undressed?" I approached Veronika. "And isn't it too dark in your glasses?"

She had a black eye. A disgusting violet bruise under her left eye. Lena came over, toweling herself. Katya angrily asked, "Igor?"

Tears streamed down Veronika's cheeks as if from a broken faucet. She didn't blink, she didn't wipe them across her cheeks, she paid no attention to them, as if they were separate from her.

"Bastard," I said.

Veronika nodded.

"Scum," Katya commented. "What happened?"

"He didn't sleep at home. I told him I was leaving." Veronika's voice was higher pitched than usual. "He started hitting."

There was no limit to our indignation.

"I took pictures afterward." Veronika began sobbing loudly. "He's not getting away with this any more!"

"Will you send him to prison?" Lena couldn't believe it.

"I don't care. Prison, wherever." She wailed and we were with her completely. "I hate him!"

I didn't know what to say. But at the moment we all hated Igor as much as she did.

"He threw me on the bed." Her voice was almost gone, she wasn't crying anymore, just whimpering like a newborn puppy. "I didn't want to frighten the children, so I couldn't scream, and he raped me . . ."

I was stroking Veronika's arm and repeating over and over, "The pig . . . what a pig."

Veronika stopped crying and put on her dark glasses. Then she took them off.

Igor looked like a good-natured caricature of Schwarzenegger. But Veronika thought he was gorgeous. That was love.

"Where did you get photographed?" Katya asked.

"I went to the emergency room. I'll tell him that if he doesn't leave, I'll go to court. I have a doctor's report." Veronika undid the cuff and pulled up her sleeve. "I have more on my legs."

She looked at her bruises in horror.

The intercom buzzed. I picked up. The housekeeper said that Veronika's husband was here.

"You told him where you were?" I couldn't believe it.

She shook her head. "It's Wednesday. He figured it out."

"Are you going to see him?" Katya asked.

"He won't go away. I might as well go upstairs." She put on her glasses and went to the door.

"Call us if you need us," Lena said.

"Want us to go with you?" I suggested.

"No. Thanks, girls."

I went into the steam room and Lena and Katya stayed to talk about Igor.

Veronika returned rather quickly. With a pleased, peaceful look. Last night Igor beat and raped her, but today he had come, crying and getting down on his knees—and that restored the balance. Veronika was satisfied. But she demanded more—it was the principle of the thing. He had to pack and get out today. Or she would go to court tomorrow.

"It's Nikita's birthday in two days," Veronika said. "A fine present for his son!"

We made her undress and get in the steam bath. A massage was impossible, too many sore spots on her body. Galya massaged her feet and put a warm compress on her face.

Lena told Veronika about the furniture and asked her advice.

"Take it all!" Veronika declared. "Even what you don't need. You can always throw it out. Or it give to someone."

"That's what I think," Katya added, and we made the decision by a majority vote. Good thing he wasn't an oil baron and too bad he didn't own a jewelry store.

I saw Veronika four days later. They had moved the birthday party to the weekend. Igor moved among the clowns and acrobats with a glass of wine and didn't look at all like an abandoned husband.

"How are things?" I asked Veronika as Masha handed Nikita his present.

"Ah," she said with a shrug. "He's a monster." She called her husband a few more names but there was no anger in her voice. "He sends flowers every day. A hundred flowers so that we live a hundred years together."

"That's nice," I said.

Veronika smiled. The bruise under her eye was covered with concealer.

People were gathered in my house. They sat at the covered table and drank without making toasts.

13.

Flames flickered and fell in the fireplace. It had snowed today.

People were gathered in my house. They sat at the covered table and drank without making toasts. Six months had passed since Serge's death. A lot of people didn't show up, but everyone I had expected to see was there.

I did not invite Svetlana. With her huge belly, and the baby floating in it, she would have been the center of attraction. Egoistic jealousy kept me from telling Serge's parents about their grandson.

My mother-in-law had an empty plate, her lips were pursed tight, and she was trying to find some inner strength. Her sorrow would grow deeper with every year.

Serge's father, a life-loving womanizer in his early sixties, drank vodka nonstop, only pausing between shots to wipe tears from his face with a clumsy hand.

I looked at my mother's still face and wondered what she was thinking about. Serge? Masha and me? Herself? Or that she hadn't covered up the garden beds at the dacha before the first snow? She caught my eye. "Have some valerian drops," she mouthed at me. It was about the tenth time that day she urged the soothing herbal remedy on me. She loved us: Serge, me, Masha, the garden, and many other things that made up her life. Nothing would make her give up hope. Her unshakable love of life made my mother invulnerable.

Vanechka called. He said some words that did not resound in my heart. We had lost each other.

"You don't appreciate what you have until you lose it," he quoted, apparently one of his latest proverbs. It wasn't clear what he meant by it: me, Serge, or all three of us.

People came and went. With children and wives. Friends and acquaintances. People I didn't consider friends but who thought they were.

It looked like an ordinary party. We drank and shared the latest news. If we hadn't seen each other in a long time, we called out in loud voices. The women sat apart and gossiped.

Life went on, no matter what.

I was standing with the men. They all wanted to know about the buttermilk. From the men's point of view, all the profits would be eaten by transportation costs. I explained the complex plan of delivery to the retailers and was extremely flattered by their attention. We discussed the advertising budget. I recommended Irma and her agency, and someone actually took down her number. I complained about the lack of technical experts, and they told me about an employment agency. When I brought up wanting to expand my market and perhaps increase the assortment, several people readily offered their services. The husbands of my girlfriends were talking to me as an equal. It was an incredible sensation.

My monopoly of the men ended when Katya came over. She had cut off her luxurious chestnut hair and was showing off her tiny skull with its soft fuzz. Its vulnerability was sexier than all the erotic magazines put together.

My buttermilk was quickly forgotten. Everyone reached out toward Katya's head, begging to touch it.

"Get ready," Regina said confidently. "Great changes await you in life." She was the wife of Vadim, Serge's best friend. She made a special point of walking near me with a glass of wine in her hand.

Regina was a screenwriter. She liked to say, "I'm like a minigod. I create a world." We weren't friends. She didn't know our problems and we didn't understand hers. Her feet didn't touch the ground when she walked, and we stood with both feet firmly planted.

Katya turned her elegant head in her direction and raised her eyebrows.

"I'm telling you," Regina said with a smile. "Something will change."

"I'm ready."

With no hair, Katya seemed more open. Was that one of the changes I was to expect? Vadim came over to me. "Well, and how are you?"

He rarely called. I wasn't hurt.

Once upon a time, when I bought cheese and yogurt for Serge's breakfast, I would get enough for Vadim as well. I don't think Regina ever gave him breakfast.

"Fine," I said and smiled. "I'm working."

"Good for you. It's working very well."

"Thank you."

We went out on the veranda and stood looking into each other's eyes. "How's Masha?"

"She's better now. Much."

He was silent and then said, "The police aren't bothering you anymore? Have they left you alone now?"

"Yes." I had forgotten about them. "I was there only twice."

Vadim nodded. "We solved that problem. They had a warrant for your arrest."

"What?" I laughed. "They wanted to arrest me?"

"Yes." Vadim didn't seem to think it was funny. "They even came to your apartment to get you, but fortunately you were at the house."

"That's horrible." Six months later, the whole business seemed unreal to me.

Vadim, on the contrary, remembered all the details and was reliving the events.

"We made a smart move then. There were two detectives on the case, one was ours completely, but the other one kept vacillating."

I recalled the station house, the interrogation, and I figured out which one Vadim meant.

"So we gave them a devil to blame. There was a warrant out for him anyway. A real viper. He'd kill you as soon as look at you. But they couldn't find him. Too bad."

The sudden guess arose not in my head but somewhere in my guts. "The computer composite picture?" Vadim would answer and it would all be clear.

"Yes, the woman was on our payroll. She said she had been walking by. We showed her a photograph, and she gave them the description. They worked with her for two hours, but she enjoyed it. The computer and so on. Technical progress impressed her. Where are you going?"

"I'll be back."

He watched me go in surprise. I walked past my guests, smiling automatically, replying automatically. I went from room to room, obsessively, looking for something but not knowing what.

I drank a neat Bacardi, went outside, and had another. I couldn't sit or lie down, or stand or walk. I seemed not to exist at all. A heavy blow had hit my mind. I think it's called a knockout. My mind had accepted it and didn't want to come out of it. It was afraid.

It was like having a worm in my head. It crawled painfully from the nape to the eye sockets, its slimy body propelled by its contractions. Monotonously, unceasingly, it spat out words I had heard somewhere today: "I am like a minigod. I create a world."

I waited for it to end. It wouldn't.

I had killed an innocent man. K.O. Take me out of the ring.

I think Katya helped me to my bedroom.

When you're twenty, you drink to make people like you—you become witty, open, uninhibited.

When you're thirty, if you want someone to take a fancy to you, you try not to drink. Because (and where does it come from?) you become sarcastic, self-confident, and—horrors!—vulgar.

At twenty you want to be closer to people.

At thirty you want to be closer to your twenty-year-old self. And farther away from people.

After a few Bacardis on the rocks at twenty the earth smoothly slips out from beneath your feet. At thirty, the heavenly vault squashes you.

At twenty, you wake up with a smile, at thirty with a headache.

I made my way to the medicine cabinet as if my head were filled to the brim with a precious liquid.

I took some analgesics. On the way back, I tripped on a pink bowl. It turned over, knocking over a mop that struck me hard on the back. There was still a pail to get around before I reached the bed.

In bed, I was safe. The silk sheets enfolded my body and gradually the rattle stopped shaking in my head. I burrowed in the blankets and regretted not keeping alcohol in the bedroom.

I listened to the sound of the surf. I was a grain of sand, one of billions. Together we made the sand. Waves moved us back and forth and tossed us onto shore. As the tide went out, it pulled us back in. I was a grain of sand that thought it was a wave.

I was a dead seashell.

I called Oleg. You always want to shift your problems onto someone else. He was asleep.

I asked him to come see me. Ever since he got a Mercedes and driver, I stopped hiding my address and phone number from him.

He was busy for the next three days. I was furious. Who'd been giving him money all these years? Occasionally. And work.

He agreed to have breakfast with me at the Palace Hotel. In two hours.

I was late, as usual.

He was waiting for me.

"What did you ask me the last time?" I attacked without even saying hello. "About some rat?"

Oleg was calm. He was drinking coffee in a tiny white cup with a black border. "Sit down," he said with a smile. "What's happened?"

"Remember, you asked me about—"

"Vova the Rat. And?"

"Why were you asking?"

"Will you have some coffee? Croissants? I've ordered an omelet, too."

"Oleg! Can you answer me?" I was losing patience.

"You first. What happened?"

A starched waiter lit a candle on the table, adjusted the flower in the miniature vase. I spoke softly. "It wasn't him . . . Understand?"

Oleg lit up, blew a few smoke rings. "I knew. The guys told me."

No miracle happened. The nightmare continued. Oleg went on.

"He said it was Vova the Rat who killed your husband."

Oleg stopped and looked perplexed. "You don't know who that is, do you?" he asked.

I shook my head.

"Then why, if he said it wasn't him, why . . . why did they . . ." I couldn't understand. And I couldn't say the words, either.

Oleg shrugged. "Do you really think that they all repent and go to confession? Anyway, it was their job, they were being paid to do it. As for the rest . . ."

He waved his hand to suggest that they didn't give a damn about the rest. Or maybe that it was all in God's hands. "And anyway, lots of people say lots of things."

I shouted at the top of my lungs: "But it's true!"

There was only one other customer, an elderly Englishman. He drank his tea with milk and paid no attention to us.

"The driver said so, too," I added in a quieter voice.

"Isn't he in a coma?" Oleg asked.

"He's out of it."

"Oh."

Oleg must have felt sorry for me. "Don't be upset," he said as if someone had just eaten my chocolate bunny. I looked at Oleg and could not believe that we were speaking the same language.

"You know," he said, a grimace of disgust transforming his face, "he was a real louse."

I tried to stop him. *De mortuis nil nisi bonum.*

"I understand that it sucks," Oleg continued, "but . . ."

I took out a cigarette. He clicked his Dupont lighter. I hadn't smoked in ten years or so. "I can return your money."

It wasn't about the money. I stubbed out the cigarette.

"When I found out who our mark was, I asked around a bit . . . it was a confluence of circumstances . . . He was in the way of a lot of people . . . What did I have to lose?" Oleg looked at me guiltily. "You're not the only person to put out a hit on him. Don't be mad."

I didn't understand whether he was smiling because he was happy or because he wanted to show off his new white teeth, thinking this was a good reason.

"What?"

"I had another client who wanted him dead. So since there was this mistake with you, if it'll make you feel better, I'll return your money."

I shook my head. "It's not necessary."

He was happy. I looked out the window. The street scene looked like an illustration for the textbook poem, "Frost and Sunshine." I ordered tea and cakes.

"A mistake," I thought, relishing the word.

The tea was so aromatic that I asked the waiter for the brand.

"Ordinary Lipton," he replied.

"A mistake."

I wanted to tell Oleg that he looked wonderful. "Get yourself a new lighter," I recommended.

"Which kind?" He squinted at his gold Dupont.

"A disposable."

"Why?"

"Only oafs use those. Or people with no money."

"Fine." He nodded amiably.

"So who is this Vova the Rat?"

"I don't know." Oleg signaled the waiter for the check.

"Are you sure it's him?" I asked.

Oleg shrugged. "What does the driver say?"

"The driver can't talk yet. He can write, and that's hard for him."

"What did he write?"

" 'Rat.' "

"Not a lot." Oleg sighed. "More information would be good. Otherwise you can end up wiping out the entire criminal class in Moscow."

I smiled. "No one would mind that."

"Depends. At least these were people we know. New ones will show up." Oleg put down his credit card without even looking at the bill. "Would you like anything else?"

"Not now."

He looked at my thoughtful face and said in approval, "Hmmmm . . . By the way, about your driver. Make sure someone doesn't shut him up forever."

"I know. He's got round-the-clock protection. He's a witness."

I believed in miracles from childhood. And as a result, I believed in God. I would secretly go off to church and ask God for miracles: an A in math, not to go to the dentist, not to be blamed for my torn dress, to get a puppy. Usually the miracles happened. I thanked God and asked for new miracles: let me get into college, let him fall in love with me, let my baby be healthy, let him buy me a 220 Mercedes.

A few months before Serge's death we were lighting candles in church at Easter, and I realized that I had nothing to ask for from God. I tried to come up with something but couldn't. I decided that that was the main miracle, when you don't need anything because you have everything.

When Serge was killed, I said to my mother, "There is no God." She replied, "Unfortunately."

Oleg's car turned the corner, but I stared after it for a long time. Someone honked the horn behind me. I stepped on the gas as if I were testing the pedal. I moved off slowly.

People were busily striding through the streets, slamming the glass doors of stores, stopping in front of the windows. The sun was reflected by the snow and blinded them, and they squinted but did not hide their faces—sunshine was so rare this time of year. Decorated Christmas trees were everywhere, garlands sparkled with colored lights—the whole city was festive, anticipating the holidays. Counting the days and hours impatiently.

I parked by the little church at the Vagankovskoe Cemetery.

There was a lot to pray about today—the repose of Serge's soul, the health of my daughter and parents, that my business may flourish, and that my soul be calm, and that the future would be—

But that's not why I was here. Not for a miracle, either. For the first time in my life I went up the steps into church to ask for forgiveness. Humbly and meekly.

We had

four nose jobs,

six liposuctions,

two eyelid tucks,

and five lip jobs

among us.

14.

I came to the office at 10:30, my usual time now. A thick file with the accounts for the last month lay on my desk. Next to it was the second account book for under-the-table cash payments. I took off my fur coat, checked myself in the mirror, and went back out to the reception room. The dispatchers were supposed to have left me a list of the stores that owed us money.

"Here it is." My secretary promptly handed me several sheets of paper. I ran my eyes over them. Ten stores were holding up payments for goods they had sold.

"Call Boris for me," I asked, and my secretary dialed the internal line. Boris was in charge of sales and I wanted to hear his solution to this problem personally.

"You do know that the advertising budget comes from revenues?" I attacked little Boris in his very large jacket.

"I know." Of course he knew, we had made up the annual budget together.

"And how am I going to pay for the billboards"—I looked at my calendar—"the day after tomorrow?"

"What am I supposed to do?" Boris was indignant. "Send thugs to beat them up? Sue them?"

"I don't know." I really didn't know. After we had expanded our consumers by another thirty stores besides the Razvilka chain, the problem of late payments had become acute.

"I threatened and begged. Nothing helps. They hold up payments weeks at a time."

"Get friendly with them," I suggested.

"All of them? There's a lot of them, and only one of me!"

"Let's create a new position—friend of store directors. He can take them out drinking once a week."

There was a commotion outside. The doors were flung open with a bang, heavy boots came trampling in, and five men carrying automatic rifles and wearing black masks burst into the office, and we found ourselves on the floor, hands behind our heads.

Through the open door I could see my secretary and a couple of employees spread out on the parquet floor. It felt as if the shooting was about to start—not just in my office, but all over the city.

I thought, *Is my skirt hiked up?*

"Who's in charge?" one of the masked men demanded.

I waited a few seconds. "I am."

My voice was hoarse and strained.

The man came up close to me so that his polished shoe was next to my eyes and he looked at me. He nodded at someone and the door was closed. "You can get up."

I rose clumsily, regretting that I hadn't worn a pantsuit that day. "May he get up, too?"

"Who is he?"

"The manager."

"He can wait outside."

Boris got up. He was huddled so tightly under his big jacket that it looked as if only a jacket was walking out the door. Three of the men in masks left with him. That left two men. And me.

"Sit down," they said.

I sat at my desk, trying not to look at the accounts.

"Who are you?" one of them asked, and I heard a note of goodwill in his voice.

I told them my name.

"So this is your company?"

"Yes."

They asked me to show our certificates of incorporation. I went out into the reception area with them. The secretary was still on the floor. The district inspector was in the doorway. He had come by once to introduce himself.

When I returned to my office, a man was sitting at my desk leafing through my papers with interest.

I thought that in these situations you're supposed to call someone, ask for help. But I couldn't figure out whom to call.

"So," he said. "We're seizing your documents."

"What for?" I understood how silly the question was as I said it.

"You probably want to know who we are?" the one in the mask suggested.

I nodded. They showed me their IDs—they were from the Economic Crimes Administration.

"And why are you here?" I asked cautiously.

"Planned check," the man without a mask explained pleasantly. The other one removed his mask. "Have you heard about them?"

I had not.

They sat down on the love seats.

"Would you like coffee or tea?" I asked.

"Wouldn't turn down a cup of tea." The older one winked at his companion.

I was about to push the intercom button when I remembered that my secretary was still down on the floor. "Could you let my people up?" I asked, smiling flirtatiously.

"What for?" the younger asked, smiling back.

"Well, so that they can make us some tea, for instance." We behaved as if we were at a picnic somewhere. The automatic rifles didn't fit the picture, though.

The senior man used his walkie-talkie to inform his people to let my staff up from the ground. But they were not allowed to move around or pick up anything.

A frightened secretary brought in a tray of tea. *She's going to quit tomorrow,* I thought.

"Well, how's work going?" the senior man asked, blowing on his tea.

"Thank you," I replied noncommittally.

"We can see it's going well." The young one looked around. My office was decorated in the glamorous 1930s Hollywood style.

"But you know, we have a lot of problems." I looked at them significantly.

"For example, the Economic Crimes Administration is going to confiscate your cash accounts."

"Do you think we could come to some accommodation?" The smile never left my lips.

"How could we do that?" he asked with feigned surprise.

We went on in that vein for an hour and a half.

"You know, you're a charming young lady," one of them said, "and you don't look like a business shark at all."

"You're very pleasant young men," I replied, "and you don't look like cops at all."

Finally we got down to business. "I have three thousand dollars US in my safe."

They laughed. "Twenty. And that's less than you would pay if we confiscate your documents and you have to stop work. For a month or so."

"Five!" I offered.

"Five will just cover our being here. How much for the documents on your desk, pretty lady?"

We finally agreed on ten thousand. I was supposed to get in their car with the money, and they would let me out a few kilometers away. My staff watched anxiously as I left.

We exchanged telephone numbers in the car, and they assured me that I had nothing to worry about for the next year.

The first person I saw when I got back was our local cop. "I offered to be friends, didn't I?" he said without preamble. "I would have warned you. But no . . ."

I reached my office and several of my people surrounded me. I looked at Boris. "Meet with the local cop tomorrow. Give him two hundred dollars as a Christmas bonus."

They wanted an explanation. "Everything's fine," I said merrily. "It was a planned check. Get used to it."

I got rid of them and closed the door. I brushed off the carpet threads that had stuck to my sweater when I was on the floor. I looked through the accounts again. I had to add another expenditure line.

I dropped into World Class without an appointment and, naturally, I couldn't get a manicure. All my pleas to fit me in at least for nail polish were to no avail. I drove to a few other salons and finally hit the jackpot. There was a no-show and they gave me her appointment.

I was getting ready for Lena's birthday party.

The middle-aged manicurist Elena was known all over Moscow. No tabloid could ever fit in all the gossip she heard in the course of a day. She had worked in all the fashionable salons, knew all the glitterati by name, and when she worked at Wella, the first lady was one of her clients. Oddly, Mrs. Yeltsin preferred to gab with the gals at the salon rather than have the stylists and manicurists come to her. Elena owed the first lady her move to a co-op studio apartment from a room in a communal flat.

She asked me what was new as she brandished her file masterfully. I could have told her anything at all, secure in the knowledge that she would never repeat it.

I simply shrugged.

"Where did you have your nails done?" she asked a bit jealously. "Look, they've ruined the shape of the pinky."

"Somewhere in Moscow, I don't remember," I said vaguely, trying not to reveal that I hadn't had a manicure in three weeks, thereby ruining my reputation.

She nodded scornfully.

I had a shampoo and she had to finish applying the polish while I sat under the dryer. They did my hair rather well, though not the way I wanted.

An hour later I walked into Bisquit, one of the most expensive and exclusive restaurants in town, with a bouquet of flowers.

Lena was having an all-girls party. I wished her a happy birthday and sat down next to Veronika. She was complaining that her sixteen-year-old daughter couldn't even make hard-boiled eggs topped with mayonnaise.

"She didn't keep them in cold water long enough, so the membrane stuck; she cut them in half the short way, so they fell over from the weight of the mayo, which revealed yellowed spots, where she had managed to burn boiled eggs. It's my fault. Where is she supposed to get any practice? We have a cook. Maybe I should send her to a cooking class?"

"Italian cuisine," Tanya recommended.

She was the daughter-in-law of the president of one of the former USSR republics. Her husband was banned in his homeland, because his father thought he would discredit him in the voters' eyes. His older brother, whom Tanya hated because of his snooty wife, was his father's right-hand man. Just like in the fairy tales.

"You're asking too much from her," said a brunette with a gold heart from Bulgari dangling from a leather strap. "How many languages is she studying?"

"Three," Veronika replied after a pause, as if she had to count them.

"What else? Music?"

"Yes," my friend said proudly as she speared a ring of calamari. "She finished music school, in piano. And the school of art history at the Pushkin Museum."

"What's she doing now?

"Applying to the Institute of Foreign Relations."

Two waiters served up some delicious-looking mushrooms.

"Well, when is she supposed to find the time to boil eggs?" Lena asked with a laugh.

Tanya was still nattering on about cooking Italian: "There's this marvelous course, it's five days. A small group, seven people. You fly to Rome on a Monday. Stay in a good hotel, and every day you have cooking class and then excursions. The chef is from a Michelin-starred restaurant. I want to go myself. And do some shopping."

She picked up her wine glass. "Let's drink to the birthday girl! May God send you a rich husband!"

We all clinked glasses.

"And so?" Veronika went back to her daughter. "So she'll make an excellent carpaccio or papardelle and won't be able to scramble some eggs?"

"Stop already," Kira said with a shrug. "Your scrambled eggs are just a load of cholesterol, anyway."

Kira stood out in the sea of pale faces with her marvelous, chocolate tan. The pampered little doggie on her lap, a Yorkshire terrier named Taya, was about the same color. Her silky fur would make a great wig.

Kira was just back from Florida, where she had taken Taya for surgery. They did it in Europe, too, but there they added miniature wheels to the back legs to make moving around easier. In the United States they managed without that.

"Wheels aren't very convenient," Kira said. "They probably make noise. And threads from the carpet could get caught in them."

The operation was a success and Kira was offering the veterinary clinic's number to all interested parties.

I didn't know the woman on my left. She owned a sport-clothing store. She picked up on the hospital and operation theme and began talking about her new boobs in a loud voice. She'd had the surgery only a month ago. The stitches weren't even healed. It was a topical subject. Half of us at the table had done it and so the conversation grew livelier. We burst into gales of laughter whenever anyone pointed out that we could be heard at neighboring tables. The restaurant was very full, a typical Friday night.

From breasts we moved on to plastic surgery in general. We had four nose jobs, six liposuctions, two eyelid tucks, and five lip jobs among us.

The toasts came faster and the conversations grew louder. It was getting close to midnight and the restaurant was gradually emptying.

Someone suggested moving on to Red Riding Hood. Lena asked for the bill, gave the waiter her credit card and the number of her membership discount card. With all the "last cigarettes" and "last glasses of wine," another half hour went by before we noisily put on our fur coats, got into our cars, and headed for the ladies' strip club.

The club was empty. We were the Red Riding Hood's only customers. We took a big table in the middle, right under the big metal cage. We were given the menu. We selected "hot dancing." Each ordered her own cocktail. We asked for separate checks, because we were drinking a lot, it was an expensive place, the bills would be horrendous, and it was impossible to keep asking one another who had the "individual strip tease" or "dance in the office." Each of us was in charge of her own bill.

Young tanned bodies in thongs danced before our table, and Lena and Katya got up to dance on the stage (for an additional charge), while Tanya fearlessly climbed into the cage, followed by a black dancer. Kira couldn't take her eyes off the blue-eyed blond in fishnet trunks who had chosen the Yorkie as his dance partner. The music was so loud that we stopped trying to talk and wandered off in search of personal delights.

About two hours later I realized that I hadn't seen Lena in a long time. I went outside to check whether her car was still there. It was. Even if she had gone off to a private room with a stripper, she would have been back by now.

I set down my mojito on somebody's table and went to the toilets. The door to the first stall was partially opened. Using two American Express cards, Olya was chopping lines of cocaine on the toilet seat lid. Katya was crouched next to it, a rolled hundred-dollar bill ready to snort.

"Have you seen Lena?" I asked.

They hadn't.

I went through the whole club again and went outside. I walked over to Lena's car. She was inside, shedding bitter, drunken tears. I didn't have my coat and I banged on the window.

"It's cold!" I said indignantly, when she finally let me in.

"Sorry," she gulped.

"What are you crying about? You're the birthday girl."

She didn't answer, just wept some more. I hugged her. "Something he did?"

She nodded. "He left for Berlin two days ago and he hasn't called once," she said, swallowing whole words.

"He didn't wish you a happy birthday?" I really was surprised.

"No," Lena said and wailed.

"Did something happen?"

She didn't reply. We sat in the car, hugging and not talking. The tears dried on her cheeks, but we didn't move.

I was afraid we'd fall asleep in the car. "Shall we have a drink?" I suggested.

"Let's," she replied. "And then let's go home."

"Okay."

We left for home at dawn. The highway police were asleep in their huts, there was no traffic, and we all made it home safely. Lena had turned thirty-two.

Her first feeble "a-a-a" sounded like an SOS in the open ocean.

15.

I regarded myself in the mirror with delight: my wrinkles were gradually reappearing. My smile wasn't completely back yet and it resembled the one clowns draw on their faces, but the progress was visible. Merry rays of laugh lines ran off from the corners of my eyes and I continued practicing in front of the mirror. Finally, one of my smiles seemed satisfactory. I memorized it. Another few minutes were spent teaching my eyes to smile.

I was pleased with the results. I liked myself again. What a terrific feeling! I was a beauty. I swirled around the room in my silk nightgown with spaghetti straps imagining that it was an evening gown and that hundreds of delighted eyes were entranced by me. I kept stopping by the mirror to flash that killer smile that so few people manage to have. I decided to have an affair with a photographer, so that I could pose for him all the time. I felt like a James Bond heroine, who could seduce anyone. An intoxicating feeling!

My mobile phone rang with the bravura theme music of a favorite cartoon show. It was Vanechka's Moscow number. I had almost forgotten him. But still, there's an inexplicable charm about people who had hurt you once. I wanted to answer, but no! He had his chance. The catchy tune was cut off in midphrase. "You don't miss the water till the well runs dry," I said, trying to find a proverb Vanechka would use. No, that wasn't it. "The cat plays and the mouse cries."

I thought about how no one had loved me in a such a long time. I tried to imagine a man whose love would be a long-awaited reward for me. My imagination kept serving up Serge to me. I tried to change the picture, but that only changed his expression. I tried to trick myself. I pictured Tom Berenger embracing me passionately. I ran my fingers through his thick curls. He bent over to whisper in my ear, his lips touching it, and his voice was Serge's.

With a sigh I took out the papers I brought home from work and buried my nose in the accounts.

I was interrupted by Lena. She wanted to know if she could drop by. I knew that if I stopped working with the numbers and percentages now, I would have to start all over again. But Lena said she was just a few minutes away, so there was nothing I could do but be happy to see her.

Lena was disappointed. No sooner had her lover returned from a business trip and made up for missing her birthday than he decided to go to Courchevel with his former family for New Year's. For the child's sake. So the girl would have a good vacation. Mother, father, and daughter—the complete family unit. Lena was furious.

"I hadn't said anything about New Year's, waiting to see what surprise he had in mind. Fine surprise." Lena fumed.

"What did he say?"

"Nothing! He says, 'but it's my daughter!'"

"Horrible," I agreed. "So what will you do?"

"Where are you celebrating?"

"I don't know yet. If my mother will take Masha, I'll go out somewhere."

"I'll go with you. The hell with him." Lena was very upset. "You know," she said a few minutes later. "I've fallen in love with him."

I sighed in understanding.

Since the last time I had seen Svetlana, her belly had tripled in size. She was huge, like a sumo wrestler, and she had stopped taking care of herself.

I was sorry that Serge would never see her like that.

We met at the Veranda at the Dacha. That was her idea. I thought that it wasn't very safe to be driving in your ninth month, especially going out of town.

She started talking about that very thing. "The steering wheel digs into my stomach," she complained with a smug air.

I suggested she take taxis.

We each ordered the tandoori chicken, and she also made a production of asking for sour pickles. The waiter smiled understandingly.

"Why won't you rent a condo?" I asked, fighting down my irritation.

"You know," she said, giving me her devoted look, "I've decided not to rent an apartment."

"Really?" I thought she had already spent the money I had given her.

"If you don't mind, I'd rather stay in this one for a while. I gave the money as a down payment for a condo in Krylatskoe. They're building a house, a beautiful one, and the air is good for the baby there." She sighed deeply, theatrically. "The down payment is fifteen thousand. You've given me ten, and if you would be so kind to me and Serge's baby . . . I need another five thousand."

"And the rest?" I asked.

"Six hundred dollars a month for ten years. If I thought this would be difficult for you, I wouldn't ask. I'll go study, then get a job. I have big plans."

I knew this was better than paying two thousand dollars a month in rent. It would be even better if she had her own five thousand dollars or if the Krylatskoe condo would be in my name, and she could live there rent free.

Svetlana rummaged in her bag and, glowing, took out a blue package. Tiny crawlers with snaps on the crotch. "Look, how adorable." The purchase made Svetlana so happy that she even looked prettier, tenderly holding the soft fabric to her cheek.

Out of the corner of my eye I could see the touched smiles of the girls at the next table. I felt so small and insignificant that I wanted to jump. "At what stage is the building construction?"

Svetlana carefully repacked her purchase. "Foundation pit," she said with a smile. "That's why it's so cheap."

"When will it be ready?"

"In two years. I found out it's a good company, they have several buildings around town. I think they'll bring it in on time. I'm already picturing celebrating little Serge's second birthday in the new apartment. I want the nursery to have a sailing theme."

I nodded. "All right. Drop by the office tomorrow. I'll let the bookkeeper know."

Svetlana squealed and kissed me on the cheek. I thought about how I had done the very same thing thousands of times to Serge. Except that he always smiled after that kiss, happy and resigned.

I did not smile. ATMs don't smile.

Svetlana ate her chicken, greedily looking at the food on the other tables.

Lena appeared in the restaurant. She shrugged off her jacket of fiery red fox into the arms of the maitre d' and ran over to me.

"I'm so glad you're here. I'm *so* hungry. And I don't feel like going home." She gave Svetlana a quick glance but spoke to me. "I'm not interrupting anything?"

I wasn't sure I wanted to introduce Svetlana to my friends. "Of course not, sit down."

Svetlana moved her purse from the empty chair and smiled at Lena. "We had the chicken tandoori."

"I can eat two! And pilaf! Boy or girl?" Lena looked politely at Svetlana's belly.

"Boy," she said shyly.

"Svetlana, Lena," I said. But Lena had already lost interest. She was having a lively discussion with the waiter, finally settling on mashed potatoes and beef stroganoff.

"Do you have children?" Svetlana inquired.

"This is my husband's mistress," I explained, enjoying her embarrassment.

"Ah." Lena smiled politely. After a smile like that, I stop speaking to people.

Svetlana pored over the menu. Lena turned to me with a question on her face. I left the question unanswered. We made some small talk.

The waiter brought strawberries flambé for Svetlana.

"You look wonderful," Lena said to me.

"Thank you, so do you. How's your great love?"

"I've given him an ultimatum." Lena poured more tea into her cup, a special collector's blend at ten dollars a sip.

"Right." I thought of a friend who had spent two years in jail under investigation, who used to say, "I'm for any form of agitation except a hunger strike." "What are your conditions?"

"I told him: make up your mind! I have nothing against your daughter. I'll be happy to adopt her, if necessary. But your wife?"

Lena stared at me indignantly, awaiting my approval. She got it.

"So, I said, first, a divorce, second, no more vacations with your ex, third—"

"He's not divorced?"

"Just imagine, he's not! They've been separated for four years, but she's holding on to him as if he were husband, lover, son, father, and a poor relative, all in one."

"That's horrible," Svetlana said, shaking her head, and Lena and I narrowed our eyes at her suspiciously.

"So I told him," Lena went on, ignoring Svetlana's words, "you can naturally drive your daughter to school or wherever, but not every day. That's what chauffeurs are for. You can see her on the weekends as much as you want, but without her mother. You can go on vacation with her—but just the two of you. Or with me. And you can't leave me in limbo. Right?"

"Right," I said. "And?"

"I told him not to call, not to come over, not to write or send telegrams until he's accepted my conditions. The white flag of capitulation is his proposal of marriage."

"You could try to make him jealous," Svetlana offered.

"Jealous?" Lena repeated suspiciously.

"Yes. Leave a flower in the car. A mysterious phone call . . ."

"Or put a business card in a visible spot!" Lena got into the spirit of things.

"Yes."

"Right."

"Or you could disappear for a couple of days. Leave your phone with your mother and she will say that Lena went home and just forgot her phone."

Lena was giving Svetlana such a delighted look that I almost got up and left both of them. "I've thought about that. And then explain innocently that I had been staying at a girlfriend's house." Svetlana nodded in approval.

The phone rang in Lena's purse. "That's him. Speak of the devil. I'll show him a thing or two." I think Lena even winked at Svetlana. I was flabbergasted.

It was the telephone repairman. Lena had made an appointment to show him where she needed more phone jacks. He'd been waiting at her house for the last half hour.

"I'm late!" Lena shouted, made hasty good-byes and dashed outside, putting on her jacket.

"What a nice woman," Svetlana said sweetly when Lena was out of sight.

"Yes," I said slowly. "Her husband left her for another woman two years ago."

Svetlana smiled sympathetically and patted her belly.

"I've got to go. Do you want anything else?" I asked dryly.

"No, thanks."

I got the bill while Svetlana looked for the coat checks. She agreed to everything with such appealing readiness that I thought, no wonder our husbands leave us for Svetlanas.

I spent every Sunday with my daughter. We'd go to the Santa Fe children's club or aboard the *Viking*, to the circus or a play. This time we were headed for the Durov animal theater, a Moscow landmark. Masha was in the backseat telling me the latest news from school: Larisa started her own site on the Internet, Katya's mother lets her use lip gloss, and Nikita, unfortunately, was very stupid. Masha smiled guiltily when she spoke about Nikita. Because she was very well brought up. Even too much so. I sometimes thought that I hadn't stopped bringing her up at the very moment when I should have. I seriously thought that good manners had become Masha's prison, the borders of her behavior and, much worse, of her consciousness. They had created a bunch of complexes called "don't, can't, shouldn't, not nice, and impossible." Combined with her truly kind heart and responsive nature, this made her extremely cautious. I hoped this would pass with time.

Masha boasted about her A in math and Prokhorov's confession of love, and then bitterly told me that the teacher had made fun of her hairdo in front of the whole class.

"Didn't Nanny braid your hair in the morning?" I asked.

"Of course she did. But in the break, Nikita hit me with his book bag. I raced after him and hit him with my pencil case, then I fell down and one of the rubber bands fell off."

"And the teacher?"

Masha looked down and said very softly, "She scolded me. And everyone laughed."

I was outraged and missed the red light. Good thing there was no policeman at the corner.

It had been Serge's idea to send Masha to a public school that taught English. I had wanted to send her to the British School. I'm sure they wouldn't have humiliated my daughter in front of the class there.

"Why didn't you leave? Why did you stand there and take it?" I was shouting at Masha.

She said nothing. I knew why she took it. Because the teacher was an adult, and you always obey adults.

I pulled the car over. "Get out," I said.

"Where?" Masha looked around. We were in the center of Moscow, by the park of the conservatory. Snow fell in large flakes and settled on the eyelashes of the few people walking in the street.

"Get out," I ordered. "Stand in the middle of the sidewalk and shout at the top of your lungs."

"What should I shout?" Masha whispered. She looked horrified.

"Just a-a-a-a-a. But very loud. As loud as you can."

"I can't." Tears filled her eyes.

"You can. You must! Quick!" I was screaming and scaring her. But I couldn't stop.

Masha stood on the sidewalk and stared at me through the windshield. I opened the passenger side window. She waited until it was completely open.

Her first feeble "a-a-a" sounded like an SOS in the open ocean.

"Louder." I said in a whisper. She could read my lips.

"A-a-a-a." she shouted, testing the sound. "A-a-a-a-a!"

The horror turned to daring and then to pleasure and incredible surprise. "A-A-A-A!" she shouted and the sky did not fall down on her head as she had probably expected.

People walked past, not paying any particular attention to the little laughing girl in a pink hat who was shouting at the top of her lungs. Prisoners who have escaped shout like that.

"All right, get in the car," I said, beckoning with my finger.

She didn't want to leave the sidewalk. Generals don't like leaving the battlefields where they have been victorious.

"Want me to shout again?" Masha offered, getting in the backseat.

"No, I don't."

I was smiling happily, and Masha, flushed and inordinately pleased and proud of herself, was ready to take on new exploits.

"Well, shall we go to the Durov theater? Or do you want to head straight for the restaurant to celebrate the victory?"

"The restaurant!" my daughter cried joyously, and only after I had made a U-turn did she ask, "What victory?"

"Over yourself."

We stopped at a store on the way. I bought Masha a huge pink bear.

"Misha and Masha," she said happily, sitting him next to her. All Russian bears are called Misha, like Teddy in America.

"Mama, Masha, and Misha," I corrected.

She smiled in understanding.

That must be a defense mechanism: his memory erased everything scary.

16.

The driver was giving his statement energetically. That morning, he came at ten to Serge's apartment as usual. He rang the bell. Serge opened the door right away. He was already dressed. The driver asked for the car keys, but Serge said he was in a hurry and would go down with him. The elevator, as in many old buildings in Moscow, stopped on landings between floors, so you always had to go up a flight or down a flight to reach the floor you needed. When the elevator doors opened, the driver let Serge go ahead of him. That saved his life. The last thing he saw was two men, one on the stairs above, one below. The driver recognized the one below—he had seen him in Serge's office a few times. He didn't remember anything else, not even the shots.

That must be a defense mechanism: his memory erased everything scary.

He learned only in the hospital that someone had shot at them and that Serge was dead. At first he refused to talk to the police, citing his condition. His doctors and relatives supported him.

But the cops, and I think I know which ones, threatened to remove the police guards if he didn't cooperate. That meant a death sentence. So the driver started talking.

He was very weak and could not get out of bed yet. Motor function in his legs had not been restored yet. But he could eat on his own now and the catheters had been removed.

A police artist spent several hours a day with him, creating portraits of suspects.

I kept wondering why they didn't shoot the driver again, to make sure he was dead, the way they had with Serge. Had someone scared them off? That would mean there were other witnesses. Then why hadn't they come forward?

I set a liter jar of black caviar on the bedside table. I didn't know whether he was allowed to have caviar. But that was the only thing I ever brought to the hospital. His family would hardly buy such expensive things. His mother still refused to greet me. Her hostile stare followed me around when I was there, so I tried to keep my visits to a minimum. Especially since he picked up the same manner of treating me, and that was intolerable. My husband was dead and he was alive, and that didn't make me guilty of anything.

They showed me pencil sketches of two men. I didn't know anyone who looked like them, but I looked closely, trying to memorize the faces and guess which one was Vova the Rat.

I thought how little I knew about my husband's work. I went only every six months or so to his office. At best. The last two weeks of his life he mentioned having problems, but I thought that the only problem was Svetlana.

I called Vadim. "I have to see you."

"Come on over."

Vadim's office was located in an old mansion on Sretenka. It was protected by the landmark commission and the state. And, just to make sure, it was also protected by armed guards. Vadim was in charge of municipal construction. Twenty years ago he had graduated with honors from Moscow State University in philosophy. And he started building right away: first, financial pyramids, then apartment buildings on the outskirts of town, and, finally, his own empire, named for his wife, Regina. There were wags who insisted that Regina had also been the name of either his setter or his hamster when he was a kid.

The walls in his office were painted with authentic sixteenth-century designs, every single inch of it covered with restored, multihued patterns. Vadim had brought in restorers from the Sergiev Posad Monastery in Zagorsk for that. He planned to restore the entire building eventually.

"Who is Vova the Rat?" I asked, settling comfortably into the wide leather armchair.

There was a time when I thought that Vadim was interested in me. Maybe that's just a male talent, to make every woman feel she's the only one.

"Is everything all right?" Vadim asked anxiously. "You're not in danger?"

"Why could that be?" I raised my voice. "What are you hiding from me?"

Vadim shrugged. "Why are you asking about him?"

"First tell me who he is."

"There was this guy. Serge liked him. They shared a love of casinos. You know him . . . no stopping him. And Vova was like that, too."

"That's it?"

"Well, they planned some business together . . . A joint project."

"What was it?"

"Why do you ask?" Vadim spoke very gently, and I had the feeling again that he was attracted to me.

"He's the one . . . who killed . . . Serge." I stumbled twice trying to say that sentence.

"What makes you think so?"

"Did he know this guy called Okun?"

"I don't know."

I thought about what Oleg had said and thought that there hadn't been another client who wanted to bump off Okun. He had simply lied.

Vadim was losing his patience. "Please tell me everything you know."

"I don't know anything." I cried bitterly. "Just that it was Vova the Rat. You, you tell me!"

Vadim didn't know much. The deal involved a large active state enterprise, of which the state was prepared to sell forty-nine percent. To the right people, of course. The question was basically settled, only a few details left to negotiate. Serge was going to be one of the shareholders. What Vova had to do with it, Serge did not know. But he was sure that it would be the most active role.

"Do you think that this happened because of this deal?"

"I'm certain."

"Then, this was good for Vova."

Vadim lit a cigarette. "Lots of people wanted that piece of pie."

"And you know nothing more?" I was disappointed.

"No."

His secretary brought in coffee. "I hadn't asked for coffee," Vadim said in surprise and then corrected himself. "Would you like a cup?"

"No, I've got to go." I thanked the secretary. She was the complete antithesis of Regina. And very charming. "So long, Vadim. Call me."

I was at the door when I turned around. I gave the anti-Regina a hard look. She understood, smiled professionally, and shut the door behind her. I came up close to Vadim.

"Why do you think they didn't shoot the driver in the head?" I asked, almost in a whisper.

I didn't have to explain to Vadim. They were smart, the boys from the luxurious offices. Otherwise, they wouldn't have empires named for their hamsters.

"Because they only needed Serge," Vadim replied simply.

I nodded and left.

All of Moscow had gone to ski.

The ones who hadn't left yet were packing, planning to leave right after

New Year's. The ones who feel the need for familiar faces and proximity to tycoons had gone to Courchevel. The rest were in St. Moritz.

Some eccentrics had gone to the tropics, but they were in the minority. But that minority had bought up all the Aeroflot flights, making it impossible to head for the Maldives, Seychelles, or Florida at the last moment. Or to get a room at a decent hotel. Much less a luxurious one.

Those who stayed in Moscow reveled in empty streets without traffic jams and treated friends like members of a secret brotherhood: "You're here, too. Excellent."

They met in restaurants for New Year's Eve. For those who can live on the Rublyovo-Uspenskoe Highway and have no desire to go into Moscow, there is the Veranda at the Dacha.

That's where I planned to be for New Year's Eve. We were a strange crowd: Katya; Lena with her fiancé, who was leaving the next day for Courchevel with his former family; Lena's neighbors, a married couple; and two gay men, Mitya and Motya, to make it a party.

We were given a table right in the middle, under a real birch tree decorated like a Christmas tree. When I came in a girl named Anya was at our table. She was waving a cigarette holder and putting her legs in fishnet stockings on Motya's lap. A few years ago she was lucky enough to have a baby with a tycoon, and now she could buy all the fishnet stockings she wanted and put her legs wherever she wanted. But the tycoon dropped her, and she had truly loved him.

The restaurant was full and the air held the concentrated expectation of fun. Gussied-up waiters poured wine, which was unlimited with the price of the dinner.

Anya kept swearing like a sailor, thinking that it was an expression of free will. Seeing us, Mitya waved to some friends and led Anya away to meet them. To give credit to Anya's sense of humor, she stayed on to amuse Mitya's friends, delicately blowing smoke right in their faces, while Mitya hurried back to say hello to Katya and me.

We were already embracing Kira. Her Yorkie did not survive after the surgery in Florida and was buried in an antique Chinese lacquer box in Kira's backyard. She came to the Veranda with a miniature poodle that she had dyed bright pink with Wella hair dye, to match her dress. The poodle, named Blondie, was a huge hit, eliciting squeals of delight from all the women.

Kira said she was waiting for Tanya, who was late because she was having a fight with her husband. That morning she had decided that her husband no longer loved her.

"Why?" asked Katya.

"I think she must have dreamed something," Kira explained.

Katya kept looking at her watch, because at midnight her bet with a tycoon was over. Last New Year's Eve, she had bet that she could quit smoking for a year. Fifty thousand dollars. At one minute past midnight, she planned to light up.

"Maybe you'll stop smoking completely?" Mitya asked.

"No, I'll smoke," Katya said, "and with such delight."

Katya was finishing up a house in Nikolina Gora, and the fifty thousand would come in handy.

It was so loud at midnight that it felt as if every bottle of champagne in the restaurant had been uncorked at the same instant. We shouted, clinked glasses, embraced, and kissed.

Everyone had friends at other tables, so the party was general and almost homey. I went over to say hello to Vika, who had smiled at me all evening from her table. She was with her children and her swimming coach. He was flawless. She was spoon-feeding him aubergine sauté.

"Going away for vacation?" It was like a password, that question. I expected the Courchevel reply. Her boyfriend, so young and handsome, would have intrigued everyone.

"No." Vika spat out her words as usual. "We're going in February, when everyone is back. I'm so tired of the crowds."

"Everyone says that, but no one ever vacations in February."

Vika's little girl ran up to the table and tugged on her mother's boyfriend's sleeve.

"I'm thirsty," she whined.

He gave her some water and smoothed her ruffled hair. She flashed him a smile and ran off with the glass.

Everyone dreams of having handsome men with adoring eyes, and Vika had one.

Zhanna Aguzarova arrived. Her face was bandaged, leaving only eye slits. "So that we don't see her blush with shame, having to perform for an audience like this," Mitya said. She started singing and people danced on the tables.

I saw Motya smoking a joint. I looked at the waiters. Their faces were politely indifferent. I reached for his smoke, but he shook his head and got a whole one from his pocket. I looked around for a light. Motya and the waiter offered simultaneously.

That was unexpected service. The last waiter to light a joint for me worked in a coffeeshop in Amsterdam.

There were no other miracles that night. I danced until five with Anya to the music of *Glitter*. I think Anya borrowed a mike from one of the group. Lena drank wine, glass after glass, forgetting that her fiancé had not proposed yet.

Looking at him, I thought that in his ordinary life he probably did not wear pink ties or drink whiskey straight. I had had a couple of bottles of champagne and thought myself incredibly perceptive. He's not at all what he pretends to be, I thought. By dating the glamorous Lena, he sees himself the way he would like to be and enjoys himself.

Tanya, with the confident movements of a woman with a good figure, moved from man to man, dancing playfully and constantly looking over her shoulder at her husband: "Do you see how fantastic I am?"

The youngest son of the president of a former Soviet republic was having a political debate with his neighbor on the left.

Kira met a man with a bright pink shirt and stood next to him, patting pink Blondie and shotgunning with the dog, trying to blow puffs of smoke into its mouth.

Katya had moved to the table of one of the main people at Veranda at the Dacha. He was a well-known jetsetter in Moscow. He covered his bald spot with a silly cap before setting out clubbing and impressed very young girls by knowing the words to songs from the time they originally came out.

Everyone left at once, leaving behind scarves, bags, gifts, lighters, and telephones.

The waiters gathered everything, trying to remember what came from which table. They knew that in the evening people would call and demand they return what had been forgotten. They gave the valuables to the maitre d' right away and he wrote down the owners' names. The waiters knew everyone.

A small crowd had formed at the exit. Several policemen were trying to organize the traffic. Because it was New Year's and because of the generous gifts they had received from the restaurant, they did not pester drunk drivers with breathalyzers.

We had all had too much to realize that the holiday we had been anticipating for a month was over.

We will be the first
generation of happy
old ladies in Moscow.
Just as we were the
first generation of
rich girls.

17.

It was a call from a man who said he was my driver's brother. I was taking it easy during the holidays, going into the office every other day, and if he hadn't called, I would have slept until two. He called at nine.

"Not too early?" he asked politely.

"No," I replied dryly, trying to figure out what had happened.

I hadn't been to the hospital in about three weeks, but I knew that the driver's health was in no danger. The money I had left the last time should last for another ten days or so.

"You've forgotten us." His words sounded like a rebuke.

"What happened?" I sat up in the bed and squinted at the open pane in the window. It was too cold to get out of the covers.

"You know what bad shape he's in."

"Can I help?"

"There's no one we can turn to but you." His family had been pushing me away for six months. What had changed now?

"We're taking him home," he explained. "His condition isn't really satisfactory, but it will be better for him to be home."

"What do the doctors say?" I asked, thinking about the police protection.

"Well, they're not against it."

"Congratulations."

"But there are . . . complications."

"Talk."

"He needs an aide, our apartment isn't really right for that, and he needs special foods now . . ."

I had the feeling he was reading from a list.

"When is he coming out?"

"In three days," he said uncertainly. Maybe it wasn't decided yet.

"I'll be at the hospital tomorrow. At three." I hung up.

Another apartment? Maybe they should move in with Svetlana. Maybe I should just take the child from her? Maybe I should go away? To Courchevel! And let them sell buttermilk, and hit the floor when men with rifles come in, and learn to repair packaging assembly lines, and . . .

I rolled up into a ball under the covers. I'd sleep some more. They were moving furniture in the living room—washing floors. I put the covers over my head, but the minute I fell asleep the clatter of dishes penetrated my hideaway. You wake up like that in a hotel if your room is right above the breakfast room. But there, those sounds are softened by the roar of the surf.

I tossed on a robe and came downstairs. "Please take all that away." Without greeting her, I pointed to the pails, mops, and rags spread all over the house as usual.

The housekeeper looked at me in surprise.

"I leave the house every day," I explained in icy tones, "and you can clean when I'm out. When I'm home, do the ironing or cook in the down-stairs kitchen, but the rooms must be cozy and clear."

I turned around and went back to the bedroom. The housekeeper picked up her pails, wiping away tears.

When I came back down, dressed, she came up to me. "You don't ap-preciate my good attitude," she said, proudly, her lips tight.

"I do, but you must understand my position." I could tell where this was going. "You work, then you go home to rest. I come here to rest, understand?"

"Are you saying that I do a bad job?" She wept. "I'm on my feet from six in the morning. I don't sit down once until evening. Your washing machine broke, I did the laundry by hand for a week!"

I nodded. I knew everything she would say.

"I spent so much time on your New Year's dress. The whole hem was dirty and there was wine or something on the sleeve."

I said nothing because I didn't care in the least what there was on my sleeve, wine or something. The important thing was for the spots to be removed. And they would be.

"If you don't like me, I should go." she said, taking off her apron.

I could have stopped her. I could have apologized, told her how good she was and how much I appreciated everything she did for me. She really wasn't too bad, especially compared to the others.

"Well, if you don't want to work," I said wearily.

"I don't. Because you don't want me to!"

I got in the car without breakfast.

I wondered if she would clean up those damned basins or just leave everything. I decided not to look for a new housekeeper until that evening.

I needed to eat something. I dropped by the office. They weren't expecting me. The staff were sitting on desks, smoking—even though I forbade it—and sharing sandwiches.

Seeing me, they put out their cigarettes and greeted me abashedly.

"Get me something to eat, please," I said, and went into my office.

The new secretary, an exact copy of the old one, brought me Japanese noodles. I ate them with pleasure without a single thought about how bad they were for me.

Boris came in with a few pages of tables. "Look," he said seriously. "Our turnover is half what it was."

"Why are you surprised? I warned you that soon everyone would be selling buttermilk. From the giants like Wimm-Bill-Dann to some tiny mom-and-pop operation."

I opened and shut my desk drawers. "The only reason they wouldn't do that is if buttermilk hadn't caught on," I explained in irritation, wondering how long before he sent his resume to Wimm-Bill-Dann. I hoped he'd wait a bit. I found Boris on the Internet, like half my staff, and naturally, he had no personal obligations to me.

"But what are you planning to do? Increase sales?"

"Of course not! How can we compete?"

I was planning to think about this after the holidays, hoping that things would work out by themselves. But Boris stubbornly waited for an answer. "I've told you before that we have to use what we have. We can start up a delivery firm. We have the vehicles, we have contracts with stores. We must make a proposal to food warehouses, there's something where we could be competitive. Have you done anything with that?"

I had been talking to Boris about this project for the last month.

"What about the buttermilk?"

"What about it?" I would never learn to behave like Catherine the Great. I didn't even have any water on my desk. "Forget about it. Move on. Don't look back. I'm not planning to give up on it yet—it can be number one twenty-five on our list of delivered groceries."

Boris sat with his head bent so low that the too-big shoulders of his jacket bunched up around his ears.

"Did you contact the warehouses?" I asked.

"Not completely," he mumbled.

"Take care of it today. I need answers in two days. Although, it's the holidays. You might lose two weeks."

I was angry with myself for not following up on this earlier. If you want something done, do it yourself. "What's the situation with the advertising contracts?"

"We need new ones. They've almost all expired."

"We won't sign new ones. Leave only the billboards. We're leaving TV. I hope you've reserved the billboards?"

"Of course." Boris nodded. Good boards go in a few days, so you have to book them in advance. "Some are even paid for already. But they're raising the prices for some addresses."

"Get a listing from other agencies. Just in case. And give them all to me. I'll choose. I think we'll leave around twenty until spring."

"Well, I'm off. I'll deal with the warehouses."

"Fine."

He was at the door when I asked, "Have we given presents to our staff?"

"Of course. Flowers, chocolates, and bonuses."

He handled that aspect very well. If anyone was sick and hospitalized, Boris sent broth in my name. "Then ask them to bring me some more food."

The clock said noon. I parked near the hospital but sat in the car, waiting for the song on the radio to end. It was Mylene Farmer singing our song, Serge's and mine. In the video, dressed in medieval men's clothing with lace cuffs, with her fiery red hair down to her waist, she sang something piercingly indifferent about war. Men on horseback fought with swords, fell from their mounts, were hit by cannon bursts, while she walked in their midst like an excursion guide. Until she fell in love with a general.

The driver looked better. He was sitting up and speaking softly. He smiled when I walked in.

There was no visible change in his mother's behavior. The man who walked toward me was his brother.

I had not brought caviar. I brought nothing.

"How do you feel?" I asked.

"Getting out," he said hoarsely. The tube was gone from his throat.

There was nothing to talk about. They were apparently expecting me to fall into a frenzy of activity in connection with his release.

"What do the doctors say?" I asked.

"Getting better," the brother reported happily.

His mother made it clear that she was doing me a favor by tolerating my presence.

"Do you all live together?" I asked.

The brother was married and lived with his wife elsewhere. My driver lived with his mother in a two-room apartment. But the brother was getting divorced. "For family reasons," he explained vaguely.

"Do you work?" I asked his mother as politely as possible.

She went on the attack. "I worked for forty years. I have a pension. They still call me on holidays to wish me well. Look at the two sons I raised! One almost died for you." She stopped abruptly and sniffed.

My driver was uncomfortable, but I realized she needed to get it off her chest. I suggested that we go out into the hallway to talk.

"I have nothing to hide from my sons."

"Get better," I said politely, and left.

The brother caught up with me on the stairs. "Please excuse her, she's suffered so much."

I nodded. "Since your mother isn't working, she will probably stay home with her son. I will pay his salary until he gets better. And I'll pay for the medicines. Please collect the receipts." I pushed his hand aside. "Good-bye."

"Why did they remove the guards?" he called after me.

That I did not know. But I had noticed the absence of a bored man sitting on a stool at the door. "I'll find out," I promised without turning around.

"Good-bye."

I stopped and looked him in the eye. "Good-bye."

He smiled in response.

He started calling me. Every day. Leaving me no choice but to discuss their family problems with him. He even offered me help. "Remember," he said on the phone, "if there's anything you need, don't be shy, just tell me."

I stopped picking up when the ID showed his number. He would call from a different phone. "Our patient sends his regards," he would say cheerfully, as if his main goal were to bring me good news as early as possible in the morning.

When he happily announced that the patient was going to the bathroom on his own, I asked him to spare me the physiological details. I put up with the rest.

Every day he wondered why I wasn't visiting them. "The patient is asking about you," he would intone.

The calls would stop for a while after he came to my office to get money for an unexpected expense, which was happening with greater frequency. About three days later, the calls would resume.

I learned from Vadim why the police had stopped guarding him. "By the time they find him and there's a trial, it might be a year. Who's going to guard some driver for a year?" he explained in simple terms. Then he calmed me: "Don't worry. Who needs him, really?"

"His brother," I thought.

The brother's calls had their effect. He wanted me to meet his niece, and I refused firmly. But he insisted I talk with him about higher education in Moscow: she was going to college. I recommended she study in the food industry. "If she does well, she's guaranteed a salary of two thousand rubles a month," I explained to the driver's brother. "It's a profession with a future."

"And what does it cost to get in?" he asked, with a broad hint in his voice.

I smiled triumphantly. "Nothing," I replied. "The institute isn't well-known yet."

I kept forgetting my mobile at work. That worried and insulted the brother. The patient worried, too. Even the mother began sending greetings.

I learned a lot about my driver's childhood. He was born with a cleft palate. Kids teased him. His parents didn't have money for the surgery. He was a good student, especially in history. He dreamed of writing historical novels. He didn't get into college—they didn't have the pull or the money. I also learned from his caring brother that their parents didn't have money for warm clothing, either, so he was always catching cold. Or for flowers for his girlfriend, so she dropped him. In other words, there wasn't any money, which is what led him on the path that brought him to the barrel of a gun (that is, to being our driver).

If we had known this sad story, we wouldn't have hired him. But he never seemed like a miserable person. He had lots of girlfriends, we paid him well, he drove his own car cheerfully, and was only out sick a few times in three years. Of course, this is not enough for a man who planned to write historical novels.

And if he had protected Serge with his own body, they would have been killed anyway. Except that they would have killed the driver first, and then Serge. With a shot in the head.

Svetlana gave birth. A boy, ten pounds one ounce. He scored nine out of ten on the newborn scale.

She went to the hospital alone, planning to be there early, just in case. But the contractions started on the road. Very weak ones. So they were very slow about doing all the paperwork signing her in.

"Do we want an enema?" the old nurse asked.

"Can we skip it?" Svetlana asked hopefully.

The nurse brought her a chamber pot and set it in the middle of the room. "Just don't strain," she ordered, and left.

Hospital gown pulled up, Svetlana was sitting on the pot when a group of interns entered. "This is where we register birthing mothers," a woman explained to them and then looked sternly at Svetlana. "You're not straining?"

"No," Svetlana mumbled.

Ten pairs of eyes stared at her. She wanted to run away, but the chamber pot was full, so she sat, ready to burst into tears.

The interns left, the old nurse came back and then took her to the second floor maternity department.

"So," muttered the young doctor as he read her chart, "you're planning a C-section?"

Svetlana nodded.

"But you're already dilated three fingers. You'll have a natural birth, in under an hour. Shall we try it?"

"But it's the uterus, a bend . . . the doctor said I need a C-section," Svetlana argued weakly.

"You have a uterus, yes," the doctor said. "You'll give birth without even blinking. Agreed?"

Svetlana nodded.

Six hours later the contractions were vicious. She wept nonstop, and she had two IV tubes attached.

"Give me a shot in the back!" she begged, whenever the pain let up for a few seconds.

"Impossible, dear," the nurse explained. "The epidural should have been done earlier. It's too late now."

"I want a cesarean!" Svetlana screamed.

They kept telling her she would have the baby any minute, but she didn't.

"Call my doctor!" she bawled. But his shift was over and he had gone home.

Two nurses were pushing an empty gurney past Svetlana. She pulled the IV needles from her arms, clambered from the bed, supporting her enormous belly with her hands, and rushed over to the gurney between contractions and climbed up, to the surprise of the nurses.

"Take me to a C-section!" Svetlana demanded, pointing to the operating room.

"Hooligan!" one of the nurses complained.

The pain swept over Svetlana again, and she rolled up as the tears spurted out of her eyes.

The other nurse brought a doctor.

"I think we need a C-section here," he said calmly, after examining her. "Prepare her for surgery."

One more needle went into Svetlana's punctured arm, this one bringing blessed relief. Twenty minutes later, Serge's son greeted the world with a loud cry.

"It's a boy. Alive," the midwife said in an everyday manner.

Svetlana slept insouciantly and deeply.

I learned that Serge had a son the next day. Svetlana called as soon as they brought her out of the recovery room.

I wanted to bring flowers, but I didn't come across a single kiosk on the way over. I was afraid of this baby. What if he looked like Serge? He most likely would.

In a way, I wanted him to resemble Serge. I thought of little Masha. I couldn't remember her face in the maternity ward, but there were photographs, and in them she looked like a piece of fresh meat. Except for the huge blue eyes. Masha was born with hair. Was Serge's son bald?

I remembered how Serge came to pick us up at the maternity ward. He was very worried and didn't want to take the tightly wrapped bundle that was his daughter.

If Serge were alive, he would be on his way to this hospital right now, and feeling the same emotions. But they would not be about me and Masha. That was much harder to accept than going to see Svetlana.

I put the hospital-supplied vinyl slippers over my boots and opened the door to her room. Svetlana was on the bed. It was strange seeing her not pregnant. She burst into tears when she saw me.

"What a horrible birth," she sobbed.

I remained in the doorway. "Where's the baby?" I asked.

"I don't know. They bring him to me. It hurt so much! The doctor abandoned me and went home. They couldn't give me anesthesia—"

"Calm down," I said. "It's just nerves. Congratulations on your son."

She nodded. "Do you want to be godmother?" she asked.

"I'll go look for him. Do you need anything?"

"Yes," she said with a pathetic smile. "Chocolates. I'm not supposed to, but I'll eat them anyway."

I nodded.

"You'll bring me some?" Svetlana double-checked.

"I'll buy some now. You have stores here."

I heard infants squealing behind a door. I went in cautiously.

"What do you want?" A nice young woman in a white coat hurried over to me.

Along the wall, newborns lay in glass containers. Like space aliens in a lab. I suddenly realized that I didn't know Svetlana's surname. But it turned out the baby had the same surname I did.

"Please let me see him!" I begged. "Just for a second! I'll put on a white coat."

I reached for my wallet, and she understood my movement. "You don't need the coat," she said. "Silly superstition."

I saw Serge's son.

He began screaming when I bent over him.

I gave the nurse a hundred rubles and left.

What I wanted was for no one to know about him. It was extraordinarily important for me to remain the only mother of Serge's only child. His only wife and his only woman.

The baby's cry rang in my ears when I was buying chocolate candy. He must have felt that I didn't need him in the least. I felt the tiniest bit sorry for him.

I asked a nurse to give Svetlana the bag with every sort of chocolate they had in the store. I didn't want to go back.

I told Katya about the baby. I warned her it was a secret.

"Does he look like Serge?" That was her first question.

"It's hard to tell." I thought for a bit. "I don't think he looks like anyone at all."

Katya nodded in satisfaction. "Does it make you unhappy that he exists?" she asked after a while.

"It makes me unhappy that Svetlana exists," I replied.

"Why don't you just forget about her?"

I nodded thoughtfully.

"Would you like to go take a look at my house?"

I couldn't say no. I got in Katya's car and a few minutes later we got to the construction site. It was on the Ilyinsky Highway, right after World Class.

"Are the steps going to be heated?" I asked as we went up the icy steps to the house.

"No," she said, waving away the question. "Lena said it wasn't necessary."

Each of us built a house and had her own opinions.

"We're changing the roof." Katya pointed to the huge, convoluted icicles along the perimeter of the house. "The heat is escaping somewhere."

The heat was on in the house and the workmen were wearing summer coveralls.

"I bought them uniforms," Katya said.

"I did, too."

I watched them lay tile. Neatly, one next to the other, with a smooth layer of glue. I noted their professionalism with pleasure.

Katya showed me the living room, combined with the dining room and kitchen. I praised the size. My kitchen was in the basement, because I hate the smell of cooking.

The large entry was filled with the pipes for the heated floor, fifteen cm apart. Sheetrock and bits of metal lay on top of them.

Katya jumped on the contractor. "Get rid of the mess! These are heated floors! Who's going to lift the tile later, if something's wrong? You?"

The pipes were quickly covered with plastic and protected with grates.

"You're not putting in both radiators and heated flooring, are you?"

"Yes, it's the entry, after all. The door will be opening all the time."

"Get rid of the radiators. I have the whole first floor with heating under the granite. Not a single radiator. It's really warm. You know that I walk around in T-shirts."

Katya thought about it. We went upstairs.

A large room with a beamed ceiling and parquet flooring was finished and clean.

"What are those hooks?" I asked, pointing at the ceiling.

"For the trapeze," Katya explained.

"Wow."

"It's the children's room."

I looked at Katya in amazement. She went over to the window. "You know, I actually do have problems with having children. They thought it was my tubes, but it's more than that. I'm getting treatment. I take pills every day and I go to have shots."

"Want me to do them for you?" I offered. "I always do Masha's shots and inoculations myself."

Katya smiled. "Well, maybe I'll drop by someday for one."

"You'll be cured," I said. "Everyone has babies, and you will, too."

I didn't ask about the proposed father. As far as I knew, Katya wasn't seeing anyone seriously.

We shut the door to the children's room. It was the first room Katya had finished.

"Why don't we go visit Lena?" Katya asked.

"Why don't we go to the Veranda? I'm starving. Or drive into town?"

We decided on the Veranda. Lena joined us in a half hour.

"I'm embarrassed to look the waiters in the eye," she whispered. "It's the same shift as on New Year's."

We laughed. "Me, too," I confessed.

"Nonsense," Katya assured us. "They've forgotten all about it."

Lena shook her head doubtfully. "The maitre d' was particularly polite as I came in."

"That's to keep you from making a big deal about it."

We ordered *plov*, that is, pilaf, for all of us.

"How's your skier?" Katya asked Lena about her fiancé.

"He calls, but I don't answer. I didn't pick up once while he was in Courchevel. And I miss him so much."

"Don't pick up."

"Of course," Katya said, "all he's thinking about is you, not his wife or the skiing. Just where's my Lena? Has she stopped loving me?"

Lena laughed. "I called Veronika, but she hasn't seen him. I wonder what the wife is doing?" Lena said with a sigh.

"He doesn't party," Katya explained. "Of course she hasn't seen him."

"Then why go to Courchevel?" I asked. "There are lots of other resorts."

"Cortina is good," Katya said.

"I like Zermatt," Lena said. "The old ladies are so charming. When I get old, I'll move there."

"The hot dogs are five dollars apiece," I warned her.

I owned Chanel snow blades, but I put them on only in extreme situations. Like the time Serge took Masha and me to the mountains.

"I won't even be able to chew by then," Lena explained. "The price of hot dogs will be as irrelevant to me as the price of dildoes."

Katya wanted to live in Paris when she was old. "I'll move somewhere on the Faubourg and spend all day on St. Honoré shopping the new collections."

I wanted to live at the sea in my old age. In a huge house that got southern breezes. With a tanned young man in a turban following me around with a folding chair.

"But really," Lena said. "By the time we're old, things will be normal here. We will be the first generation of happy old ladies in Moscow. Just as we were the first generation of rich girls."

"Yes," Katya agreed. "Remember before how the restaurants were filled with twenty-year-olds? Twenty-five, tops."

"And now," I said, "you can't even go to a nightclub without running into Veronika's daughter. With her friends. And you feel like a teenager at a kiddy show."

They brought our food. We made a date to go to a restaurant Friday night. In Moscow.

I had a Filipino maid now. Small and tan,
she spoke English and probably Tagalog.
She asked for a uniform.

18.

They arrested Vova the Rat. He was being held in custody and refused to give evidence.

I could not forget for a single moment that there was a place where I could go to see my husband's killer. I was glad he was in there.

They needed the driver to identify him. He could not go because of his condition.

Vova's lawyer visited the family. He had no doubts about the witness's clear mind and good memory. He simply offered them money.

The brother let me know. "That guy offered us money," he declared dramatically as he came into my office with a broad smile.

I'm sure that no one had ever offered them as much money as frequently in their entire lives as in the last six months.

"Did he threaten you?" I asked.

"Of course not," he replied, flexing the muscles of his strong neck to show how silly my idea was. "That shrimp?"

Boris peeked into the office, saw that I was busy, and shut the door.

"Twenty thousand dollars," he said suggestively.

Cheaper than murder, I thought. "And you refused the money?" I said, with naïve delight.

He looked at me in bewilderment. "Of course, we refused." And then he said, stressing every word: "You want him behind bars, don't you?"

I pressed the intercom and asked for tea. I leaned back in my uphol-stered armchair. Then I asked, as if it were an afterthought, "Would you like some tea, too?"

"I wouldn't refuse."

I nodded. "And don't you want him behind bars?" I asked thoughtfully, looking at my visitor vaguely.

He squirmed in his chair. "I would like to strangle him!" he informed me.

My secretary came in and stopped in the middle of the room. There were two of us and only one cup of tea. I nodded toward the brother, to let her know the tea was for him.

"Have mine," I permitted.

"Shall I bring more?" the secretary asked.

"No, thanks."

And then I changed the tone, going back to the way we had been talking recently. "Well, and how is the patient?"

"Fine. Reading a lot. And watching movies."

The unwritten rules of our game called for me to offer some cassettes. "I have a lot of films on tape. Would you like me to bring a few next time?"

"If it's no trouble."

"No trouble at all." I stood up. "Please excuse me, I have a lot of work today."

He put the cup, still full of tea, on the table. He gave me a hopeful look. I smiled broadly.

"Well, good-bye, give my best to everyone."

I left my office, indicating to my secretary to show him out. I shut the door of Boris's office firmly.

"So, how are things?" I asked him with a sigh.

He was flushed with excitement. "We're totally competitive on price! Just as you had predicted."

A smile spread over my face.

"Two warehouses are ready to sign. Three hundred sixty items in one and three twenty in the other! A total of six hundred and eight products to be delivered!" He regarded me with respect.

I felt like a serious businessperson. I could have lived my entire life without knowing I had this gift.

"Sign contracts," I ordered, "and raise the cut for the expeditors if they make arrangements with the stores themselves."

"But if we increase the number of stores we work with, we'll have problems with transport," Boris countered.

"Let the dispatchers stay within their regions."

"Okay." Boris nodded, then added, "But . . ."

"What?

"We won't have the same turnover as before," he said regretfully.

"But no investment, either. Don't be greedy."

"I suggest holding off on signing the contracts." Boris scratched his head, and then his ear.

"Why?" I was surprised.

"Well, we won't be able to work with every warehouse that wants to work with us, right?"

"Of course not. We have limited resources."

"So, I think we should wait until we hear from the other warehouses. They might have a bigger assortment."

"All right. Just don't drag it out. We lowered our turnover on the buttermilk to keep things moving."

He headed for the door at his usual jog.

"Why didn't you give him money?" Lena demanded when I told her the story about the driver over the phone that evening.

"I don't know." I really didn't.

"He'll retract his statement," she said with great certainty.

"Maybe he won't. The man shot at him, after all."

"I don't know." She sighed doubtfully. I pictured Lena, suspicion frozen on her face.

"Let them do the right thing, altruistically, for once in their lives," I said, not believing a word of it.

"Of course, who wants to spend twenty thou?"

"Right."

"Well, we'll see. But you have to understand that he doesn't think about Vova the Rat, who shot him. And accidentally did not kill him. He thinks, 'I was working for Serge and I suffered. And now his wife won't let me make some money.' In fact, you're expecting him to work for you for free."

I understood. It must be wonderful to have someone do something for you for free.

"How's lover boy?" I asked, changing the subject.

"He calls every day. I don't pick up." Her voice grew more animated and coquettish. "He's inundating me with his SOSes. I'm the queen of his life, he says."

"Terrific." I was truly happy for my friend. "You don't respond?"

"No, I do not," she sang.

"Good."

There's a song with lyrics that go something like: "If he comes over, I'll go away, if he smiles, I'll turn away." I don't remember exactly.

I had a Filipino maid now. Small and tan, she spoke English and probably Tagalog. She asked for a uniform. I called Majordomo, that agency that put its cards all over our neighborhood. Svetlana, the wife of Valdis Pelshe, handled uniforms. When we walked in the door, she suggested a pants suit for her.

"She probably doesn't shave her legs," Svetlana said matter-of-factly, and we both stared at the Filipina's legs. She smiled nervously.

"She shaves," Svetlana said. I thought maybe they just weren't very hairy, but I didn't want to go into it.

Svetlana drank coffee from a small antique cup while her seamstresses measured my housekeeper.

I had gotten the Filipina through a friend. The wife of a famous singer had set up an agency for Filipino maids, who are considered the best in the world, but some problems in our laws kept her from making the agency legal.

"I wonder if I should get a uniform for my masseuse?" I thought aloud.

"Of course," Svetlana said firmly. "Do you have a cook?"

"No." I shook my head.

The manager of Majordomo looked at me with condescension. "Then who does the cooking?"

"I do," I lied. I don't know why, and shrugged with a smile, as if apologizing for such primitive behavior.

Svetlana gave me a pitying look, and when we were leaving, shook my hand encouragingly.

I didn't pick them up at the maternity ward. That event was bound up in memories of bustle and excitement and a festive mood. Serge and Vadim, Lena and her then-husband, Veronika without Igor (they were fighting), and my mother all came to get us. Mother was in charge.

I did not want to be in a crowd of Svetlana's girlfriends and discuss whether everything was fine with the young mother and her firstborn. I doubted that I could be sincerely thrilled by how good they looked. Or cry out: "Who does the baby resemble? Look, he has his mother's eyes." And have some girlfriend of Svetlana's, in a short fake-fur jacket ask, "Do you know the father?" And another one—God forbid—say in a dreamy voice, "He was such a fantastic man. They had a wonderful relationship."

"I'll give you a call," I promised Svetlana, "and I'll bring things for the baby. Don't buy a tub, I have one."

I hadn't thrown or given away anything. Serge and I always knew we would have another child.

Of course, we had thought I would be the mother.

My mobile rang. It didn't show the number. I didn't feel like answering. It was late, and I could have been asleep.

"It must be Svetlana," I thought. "Here we go. The baby is screaming and she doesn't know what to do."

"Hello." It was Lena. She was whispering and speaking fast. "He's back from Courchevel. I answered the phone and told him that I was at a party. And he's come here, ringing the doorbell. What should I do?"

I didn't understand. "You're home?"

"Yes, yes," she whispered. "I just told him that I was at a party, so that he would be jealous, and he came here!" She was screaming in a whisper.

"Well, don't open the door, since you told him you're at a party."

"But my car is outside. I couldn't have walked to a party."

"So what?" I was calm and hoped my strength would pass to her. "You could have gone with Katya or me."

"Right. I'm not opening up. But I really want to. I missed him!"

Dial tone.

I would not have opened the door. Anyone can open the door when her lover is ringing the bell. But to have the willpower to wait until he's ready to knock down the door, to knock down mountains to see you . . .

The phone rang again. *He must have left,* I thought.

"How's it going, partisan girl? You didn't open up?" I said into the phone.

There was a brief pause. "Are you playing war games?" It was Vadim.

I laughed. "Yes, a girlfriend was calling."

"They released Vova the Rat."

"What?" I forgot all about Lena.

"Your driver recanted his evidence. He said he wasn't well when he gave it. The lawyer paid bail, and Vova is out."

Vadim spoke in clipped sentences. "Our cop called me. They're furious, their whole case fell apart."

"And what now?" I asked glumly.

"I don't know." Vadim sighed. "He's their only witness. They must have scared him off. Or paid him off."

"Yes." That was all I could say.

"Don't worry," Vadim said gently, as only he could.

I envied his Regina. She could hear that every day. "Don't worry," instead of the trite, "Good morning." "Don't worry," in the evening, and of course, "Don't worry," instead of the boring, "How was your day?"

I called my "pal," the driver's brother. It was the first time I ever initiated a call. Good thing I hadn't tossed his number.

"How are things?" I asked, not knowing how to begin.

"Getting better," he said evasively.

There was a silence. "Did your brother refuse to testify against the killer?" I asked.

He did not reply. I wanted to say, "Hello?" to test the connection. But I knew there was nothing wrong with it.

"I want him to testify against the Rat," I demanded. "Otherwise I'll stop giving you money and helping you out."

"That's between you and God."

I pictured his pocket red with the heat of twenty thousand dollars American. Green and crisp. Maybe still in bank wrapping.

"Don't think that we took the money," he said.

I was taken aback. It's creepy when someone reads your thoughts. "Then why did he refuse to testify?" I asked.

"We didn't say anything to the lawyer then," the brother explained, without his usual kidding tone. "He left a phone number. But we didn't call. We were waiting for your decision . . . We didn't know there was a rush."

"And?" I stopped breathing to hear him better.

"Today we got a photo of Serge in the mail. With a bullet hole in his head."

"What?" I didn't understand. The name "Serge" did not fit in any way with words like "bullet hole." Each time it was like hearing it for the first time. It caused incredible pain.

"Did you call the police?" I asked, just to say something.

"The photos came from the police. From the file. So what's the good of calling the police?" He sighed in a doomed way. "But maybe it will be all right now. They let him out, I heard. The lawyer called to thank us. Bastard."

"Can you come by my office tomorrow?"

"I'll be there." He sounded happier.

I hung up, and the phone rang again. It was Lena.

"He left one hundred and one roses at the door!"

"Did you count them?" I asked dubiously. I thought it would take a long time, one hundred and one roses. I had gotten bouquets like that once upon a time, but I couldn't remember when anymore.

"Of course. A hundred red ones and one yellow. What do you think the yellow rose means?" she asked anxiously.

"I don't know. Maybe one separation, while they were in Courchevel, and a hundred meetings. Or a hundred years together."

Lena was practically purring with pleasure. "Probably."

We wished each other a good night and went to bed. I lay in bed with open eyes for a long time. I thought Lena wasn't sleeping, either. She was guessing the meaning of the yellow rose.

I went to the office. It was a Friday. Three of my staff were bringing packages of buttermilk to the seniors in our building. We rented office space on the ground floor. The old people complained about our cars. They sent letters to various agencies. But a weekly packet of buttermilk was enough to make them put up with us.

My driver's brother was waiting for me. "I'm sorry it all happened," I said right off the bat. I sat at my desk, took papers out of my bag. And suddenly, I said in a piteous voice, "Let's put him behind bars."

He shook his head and looked at me as if I were crazy.

I leaned over the desk toward him. "I'll hire bodyguards. Armed. Twenty-four seven. Nothing will happen to you."

He looked at me suspiciously. There was fear in his eyes.

"I guarantee it," I insisted.

"No, thanks," he said, as if turning down seconds at dinner. "We've had enough."

"He almost killed your brother." I tried to play the revenge card.

They thought it was all Serge's fault.

"It's dangerous, after all." I thought I could scare them. "He'll be on the loose and thinking that his freedom depends on you. Think about it. Sooner or later, he'll get tired of that."

He looked at me with hatred. I took out my final argument. Ten thousand dollars, in bank wrapping. "I'll pay. I will cover your emotional pain. You'll get a new car. And vacation in Turkey." I held onto the money. He never took his eyes from it.

I knew that seeing actual packets of cash has a stronger effect than virtual numbers.

He kept silent, badgered.

"You'll have guards. Nothing to fear," I pressed.

"I have to talk to my brother," he said.

I extended the money toward him. "Take it."

He hesitated. "Take it," I insisted. "If you decide differently, give it back."

He took the money and held it in his hand.

"Where do you work?" I asked.

"Furniture manufacturer. We make cupboards."

"Maybe you'll want to change professions. I think we can work well together," I said encouragingly.

I shouldn't have made the offer. He almost dropped the money. "And if you don't like the idea," I hastened to reassure him, "we'll put the bastard in jail and pass like ships in the night." I thought about Vanechka. All proverbs made me think of him. "We'll call each other on New Year's to wish each other well."

He had to find the idea of being friends with me flattering. He put the money in his pocket.

"Give the family my regards," I said gently. "The guards will arrive at nine tomorrow. They'll tell you they're from me."

I smiled blindingly. He was still in the doorway. "Are you saving receipts for me?" I said, remembering.

"Yes." He nodded.

"Don't lose them," I said severely. "Medicine is so expensive nowadays."

He left.

I went to the window. Large snowflakes made the street look like an illustration for a Christmas story. The gray wolf should not stalk the woods eating whatever he wanted. Every granny needed her own Little Red Riding Hood.

I called the director of the bodyguard agency Serge used. "What would it cost to have an armed bodyguard round the clock?"

"Are you having problems?" he asked.

"No, but the witness who is going to testify against Serge's killer may have problems."

"Got it. I don't have any men now. But I'll go myself, for this. I'll find good people for you. You want them to work twenty-four hour shifts every other day or every two days?"

"Every other day. They'll get paid more and they'll care more."

"My guys are the best. They're all back from the war. How long do you think this will take?"

"Until they arrest him again. If he's not on the run, it might be a few days."

We came to an agreement. One hundred twenty dollars a day.

I went home to change. The girls and I were dining at the Vogue Café.

"You've left already?" Boris asked on the phone, when I was already in the car.

"Yes."

"I didn't get to tell you the other bad news."

"Can we do it Monday?" I asked. "No one's going to die, right?"

"No," he said, laughing as if I had made a joke. "But still . . ."

I hung up.

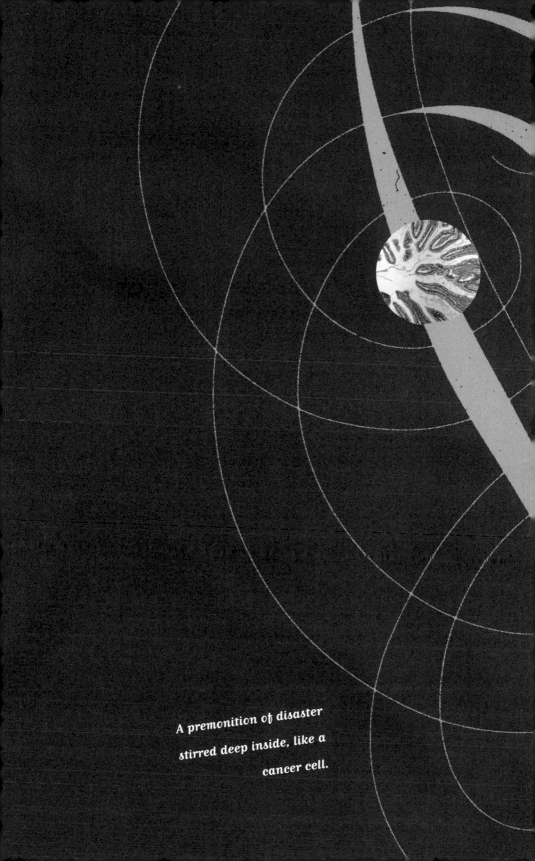

A premonition of disaster
stirred deep inside, like a
cancer cell.

19.

"How about a massage?" I asked Galya as I came in the house and looked around for the Filipina. There were no visible signs of her presence.

"She's around here somewhere," Galya said, to calm me down.

The living room was clean and even the photographs on the curved console of black wood were in the order I usually put them.

"She didn't dust under them," I decided, and tested with my finger. There was no dust.

It's amazing how something that silly can improve your mood.

Galya and I discussed the pros and cons of Philippine cuisine and went up to my bathroom. The candles were lit and a towel spread on the massage table, compliments of my new maid.

I stopped in surprise at the door.

"Massage is the same in every language," laughed Galya.

I envied foreign women. They could all have Filipino maids.

I drifted off during the massage. I pictured a white house with white furniture and rugs. The sound of surf rushed into the open windows and doors. I wandered through the rooms in a swirling dress, and no sooner did I think of something than an invisible servant presented it to me. I was bored, and I nurtured that boredom, enjoying the knowledge that it would be like this tomorrow, and the day after, and always.

———

"Are you on the way?" Katya shouted into the phone.

"No, I'm still dressing."

I took the first jeans I saw on the shelf. If you want to be in a fashionable place, you simply have to go to Arkady Novikov's latest restaurant.

The steps at Vogue Café were not heated, just like Katya's house. Thank goodness for the young man who held me and kept me from slipping. He was around twenty. I wanted to smile in thanks, but I didn't know what kind of smile it should be. Maternal, from the height of my advanced age, or flirty—he was cute. As a result, I didn't smile at all and, depressed by that, I made a haughty face and entered the restaurant.

"What a bitch!" he must have thought.

The restaurant was full. In the first room, the café, anxious girls pretended that they were really there to play backgammon. There were also tables with checkers and chess. They were occupied, too.

I went through the café, looking over people's heads for friends. None. Whatever.

Lena, Katya, and Tanya were waiting for me in the restaurant. Tanya was showing off a beautiful mountain tan. Most of the people there had one, as well. The fashion for a healthy color was catching on.

"Where's Veronika?" I asked.

"Her little Nikita is sick," Katya explained. "Reacclimatizing after Courchevel."

I ordered a fish carpaccio and a glass of white wine on ice.

"What's new on the slopes?" Lena asked Tanya.

Tanya pursed her lips. "It was fun. *Le tout Moscou,* as usual."

"And the skiing?" asked Katya, knowing that Tanya didn't know how to ski and spent the whole day in the café.

"Not bad. My husband was pleased," she replied with dignity.

We chatted in the same spirit until the waiters brought our hors d'oeuvres.

"Oh, my!" Katya suddenly said and then whispered to Lena. "Don't turn around."

But Lena was already looking in that direction. Lena's fiancé stood in the door with a plump, freckled woman.

"All right," Lena said cheerfully. "Did he see us?"

"I don't think so," I said, watching them be seated at a table.

"Just this morning he swore his love to me," Lena laughed.

"What are you so happy about?" Tanya asked.

"He's brought her here to talk to her about a divorce, I think. First some wine to soften her up. You should have heard him crying all this month. Sobbing with love. He gave me a ring. I forgot to put it on. Two and half carats."

"Are you kidding?" Tanya cried.

"Yup." Lena smiled in satisfaction.

"Is it beautiful?" Katya asked.

"Very. It's pink gold, with really heavy claws to hold the stone." She bent her fingers in an attempt to show what the ring looked like.

"Terrific," I said.

We drank some wine.

"Look, he went over to talk to someone." Tanya indicated where Lena's fiancé was talking with one of his friends.

"Let's go." Lena pulled me by the hand. "Pretend we're going to the toilet."

I followed Lena among the tables until I bumped into her back.

"Hi." I heard Lena's sultry voice and also smiled—after all, we had spent New Year's Eve together. His eyes skimmed over Lena, then me, and then someone behind me, smiled vaguely, and then turned back to his friend. "Well, let's get together this weekend."

Lena turned bright red. I noticed the attentive stare of the freckled woman, so I pulled Lena away and, smiling at everyone, moved toward the bathrooms.

"Did you see that?" Lena exclaimed.

I made sure there was no one else in the bathroom.

"It's his wife," I said.

"He didn't say hello to me. What do I care if it's his wife or mother? He sleeps with me every day. She's no wife to him, anyway!"

The door opened and a girl with a mobile came in. "Yes, I'm at Vogue Café. It's full! Yes, there are some cute ones." She threw a suspicious look at us and locked herself in the stall. "Come over, I'm waiting."

Lena was weeping silently. "Bring my coat check tag," she asked. "I'm not going back there."

I left with her.

He called an hour later. Lena did not pick up the phone. She shook her head silently. He called again.

"He must be hiding in the pissoir," Lena said with revulsion, finishing her sixth vermouth on ice. "I don't want anyone swearing love to me from a pissoir."

She liked the word. She said it a few more times while we drank. I think that when she fell asleep, that was the place where she sent her fiancé.

I pulled out a suitcase with Masha's clothes from the storeroom. I went through the tiny crawlers, bonnets, and mittens. The three-month denim cap Serge and I bought in Paris, when I was pregnant. And these funny pants with gnomes, from a common store, were bought by my mother-in-law. We probably never used them once. But now they seemed adorable.

"What are you doing?" Masha asked, peering curiously into the suitcase. Like all children, she was not indifferent to her past.

"Just looking," I said vaguely.

"Do you want to give them to someone?"

I'm always amazed by children's perspicacity.

I sat down on the floor and hugged Masha. "She's got a brother," I thought, "and she would probably be happy to have him."

Most of her things were pink. I set them aside and picked out the ones that weren't.

"You don't like pink?" Masha asked, trying to pull on a tiny knit hat.

"It's for a boy," I explained. "Would you like a little brother?"

"Nope," Masha said firmly.

"Fine, then."

I loaded the tub, bottle warmer, sterilizer, carriage, a bag of pacifiers, an electronic scale, and a baby travel bag. I packed the clothes neatly in a bag.

"Will we go to the club tomorrow?" Masha wanted to be sure.

"Of course."

She waved and went to the neighbors, to visit her girlfriend.

Svetlana's mother was at her house. She was in the kitchen, on the only stool, sipping tea loudly.

I looked at the crib. The wrinkled monkey face elicited no emotions. It was hard to imagine that this could turn into Serge's face.

"Isn't he adorable?" Svetlana asked lovingly.

I looked into her eyes. She seemed to mean it.

"Yes, very sweet."

"Just like Serge. Don't you think?"

I was trying to come up with an answer, when Svetlana's mother yelled happily from the kitchen, "Sveta! The scale you wanted, it's here!"

"Oh." Svetlana literally jumped with joy. "I'm nursing and I need to weigh him."

"Electronic," her mother shouted from the kitchen, as if the kitchen were on the first floor and we were on the fifth.

"Did they have electronic scales back then?" Svetlana asked.

I felt like the mother of a wooly mammoth. "We got it abroad," I muttered.

They bustled over the clothes, washing some things on the spot, and forgetting all about me. The baby woke up and cried.

I picked him up. He seemed lighter than Masha's dolls. I had forgotten what it felt like to hold a newborn.

Svetlana took him from me and put him to her breast. The violet, blurred nipple was the size of his face. I went to the kitchen. Her mother was smoking, trying to get the smoke to go out the small opened window pane. It wouldn't, and she had to wave her hand to dissipate it.

I imagined Serge as her son-in-law. She would quit smoking, first thing.

"That is a fine gal," she said, apparently about her daughter. "She's doing it all herself: making money and having a baby."

She spoke with respect that I would be unlikely to get from my mother in similar circumstances.

"Eh," she said, either as a question or as a statement, and I was afraid that she wanted my approval for Svetlana, too. Her mother must have thought I was one of Svetlana's girlfriends. "She's buying an apartment, and you know how expensive that is." The butt flew out the window. "She was like that as a child. When she wanted something, you couldn't talk her out of it. And life is so hard." Her eyes narrowed, checking me for signs of a hard life. She sighed. "And she doesn't abandon her mother, either."

The baby's unhappy squeak came from the bedroom. "She fell in love with someone and had a baby. Alone. That's love. And now, he's dead."

"Killed," I corrected her.

"Seryozha is asleep," Svetlana said, tying her robe.

Don't call him after Serge! I wanted to shout. *That name has nothing to do with this baby, this kitchen, that horrible robe.* What I said was, "Well, I'm off." I said good-bye and left.

I called Lena from the car. "How are you?"

"Fine."

"Did he call?"

"That doesn't matter. Forget him. I have."

She spoke seriously and a bit sadly. I believed her.

"That's right. You'll have a million others. They'll be lined up for you."

"Yes."

My driver's brother called. "We gave testimony," he announced. "And your bodyguards have arrived."

"Wonderful."

"They will have a warrant for his arrest on Monday."

"Thank you."

I woke up in the middle of the night. My left side felt as if someone had put a hook into it and was twisting it. I couldn't get up. I couldn't straighten up. I barely made it downstairs to the medicine chest. I took some painkillers. Two hours later, I took another dose.

The only thing I could do was weep. The pain would not let up.

Dawn came.

I had consumed the entire pack of pain killers, going way over the recommended dose.

I called information on Bee-Line, my cell service. "How do I get an ambulance?"

They had their own. They brought me to the Central Kremlin Hospital.

I had a kidney infection.

I was shuddering with cold. My temperature was 103° F.

It stayed that high for four days. I was so exhausted that if amputating a leg would put an end to this, I would have sawed it off myself.

They said I needed kidney surgery. "Otherwise we'll lose the girl," I heard the doctor say. They gave me forty minutes. If there was no improvement, they'd start the operation.

Forty minutes later, the fever broke. I fell into the release of healing sleep.

By Thursday I felt better. My mother, who had been in the hospital with me the whole time, went home. On Friday I asked for a television and a phone.

No one picked up for a long time at the office. It would have been better if they hadn't picked up at all.

Boris had run off. The rumor was that he had gone to Wimm-Bill-Dann.

I'm not sure what the second bad news was that he didn't tell me, whether it was that he was leaving or that the Lubertsy dairy, our partner, had been shut done by the health inspector.

"It's all the fault of your buttermilk," the dairy's director yelled at me over the phone. "Whose blacklist are you on?"

"Do you have a fax?" the bookkeeper asked me. "I'll send you the figures. We're suffering huge losses."

I looked around. I had a bed, a nightstand, and a television set on top of it. There was no fax.

"Release me, please," I asked the doctor, trying to look as healthy as possible.

"Sure," the doctor replied, "in a month or two. The next three weeks you're in bed. Do you realize how close you were to death?"

I stayed in bed for a week. The regular rhythms of hospital life were good for my nerves. The biggest event that could happen in there was a cockroach in the bathroom.

The day started with pills and ended the same way. The patients were very happy to see visitors, peeking into their bags of food. They made phone calls in comfortable leather chairs in the hallway, and they were in no hurry to go anywhere.

I wanted to get out of there as soon as possible. I felt that life was passing me by.

The bookkeeper called me every day. A lot of people had stopped coming to work. I asked her to call less often. The numerical progression, rather, the regression, was stable and I could do the math myself.

Lena came to see me.

I offered her a chair right away, remembering how uncomfortable I felt standing at the driver's bedside.

She had broken up with her fiancé. "I must be unlucky," she said glumly, trying not to look at my specimen jar. "I asked my ex to increase my allowance, since everything is more expensive with that stupid euro, and he said he was having difficulties." She sighed. "He's having difficulties, but she's not. Veronika saw the Van Cleef & Arpels jewelry he gave her for Christmas. I got a pen from Bulgari. What does he expect me to do with it?"

"But he left you the house." I came to the defense of Lena's former husband.

"I'm not wishing anyone evil, but I'd like to see him live on two thousand a month, which is what he gives me," she said angrily. "Bum. If I were a man, I wouldn't give him a thing."

I burst out laughing. "Even if you were the one who left him?"

"Right." She nodded firmly. "Think of all the pain he caused me before I left him."

"You're not fair," I sighed.

"I know that. I just need more money."

My mother brought Masha to see me. She stared worriedly and was ready to stay with me in the hospital. "You don't have anything that hurts, do you?" she asked touchingly.

"No. I just have to lie in bed."

"Your Filipina," my mother complained, "keeps asking for groceries that can only be bought at Stockmann's."

"Well, teach her to make *pelmeni.*"

"I've taught her to cook borscht. With sour cream. She tried it, and she had stomach problems for three days. They're all so sensitive."

Then Katya came. She was completing her infertility treatment. "I have to go for shots every day. I'm sick of it," she fumed.

"As long as you get the result you want."

"I can't stay long. I'm on my way to the precinct to change my passport. You know those new passports?"

"Yes. I know a girl who got the clerk to change her date of birth for a small consideration."

"Really?" Katya's eyes lit up. "I want to do that, too. Take five years off. How much do you have to give them?"

"I don't know. Try a hundred dollars."

"I'd pay two hundred for that."

I was eating my clear broth, as per doctor's orders, when my driver's mother called. I didn't understand who it was at first. All I heard were sobs, howls, and the sounds a dying person makes when they take away the oxygen.

A premonition of disaster stirred deep inside, like a cancer cell.

Their car had been blown up in the night. Its charred remains were on the street in front of their building.

The driver had given his evidence on Friday. The warrant for Vova the Rat's arrest was ready on Monday. But he was not yet arrested, and he had skipped out from his known address.

"We get threats on the phone," his mother sobbed. "They said that they would break one of my fingers every day until we take back the statement."

She was so frightened that it made me scared. I curled up in the bed and felt so vulnerable that I wanted to hide under the covers.

"Talk him out of it," she wept.

"Who?" I couldn't imagine how I would be able to talk to Vova the Rat.

"My son! He won't take it back."

The air in my tiny room felt fresher. I was not alone. Somewhere out there, surrounded by medicine bottles and specimen jars, just like me, was a man who thought the same way I did. And without knowing it, was supporting me when I needed it most. My driver.

I remembered how angry he was once with the parking attendant at a casino. He almost got into a fistfight with him. I told the story to friends with a condescending chuckle. The way you talk about your child who likes to clink his juice glass with your guests for a toast.

Now I could picture his hands making fists, color rising in his face, as he tells his mother, "No. I will not."

"Calm down," I said. "And don't go out of the house. As long as you stay inside, you're safe."

I asked to speak to her son. "Hello," he said calmly.

"Do you need more security?" I asked.

"No. They won't come into the house. We've got one in the apartment, and another outside. And a supervisor comes by once a day."

I nodded. Of course, he couldn't see me nod. "I'll come up with something," I promised. "I know," he replied, and I think he was smiling.

I got up and very slowly, very carefully, I started walking. Fear of pain made me double over.

"Where do you think you're going?" the nurse in the corridor barked.

It was February outside. I didn't know where my clothes were.

I leaned against the wall and slid down to the floor, like a drop of raspberry jam on the side of the jar. But I didn't leave any traces. They caught me under the arms and put me back in bed.

The phone rang. Every ring, strident and demanding, created horrible pictures in my mind. Blazing cars, an open elevator door and gunshots, the suffering face of an old woman whose fingers were being broken . . . I picked up the phone to put an end to the nightmare.

It was the bookkeeper. Apologizing profusely, she informed me that the bank had sent two letters already. The last payment was long overdue, and they would start taking measures over the collateral. Should she bring the letters to me?

"No." I thanked her politely.

Did I have any other questions? Yes. "What's the mood of the staff?" "Everyone's waiting for your return," she said evasively. And she asked if she could pay their salaries.

"Of course." I had forgotten that it was the seventh of the month: people had to be paid so that they could bring money home to their families, buy food and warm clothing. And some luxury item, like a real T-Fal frying pan.

"What about the brokers this month? They haven't been working. Should we give them a small sum in advance of future work?"

She hesitated. "Most of them have quit. They need to earn money. Production is at a standstill. There's no one here in management. And when he left, Boris said—"

"It doesn't matter," I said, interrupting her. "Just don't you leave for now, all right?"

She reassured me on that score. Without too much optimism, however.

It felt as if the world had spat me out into the garbage bin.

By the following Monday, I could walk. Trying to hold my back straight. Even though bed rest was the recommended pastime.

I was allowed to go home when I signed a release. Veronika picked me up.

"You need a driver," she said loftily.

A friend of hers had opened Nikita, an agency for female bodyguards. I could pick one with a driver's license.

"Why do I need a woman?" I queried.

"Well, she won't stink up your car. And you can find a nonsmoker."

I pondered. Veronika called her friend and told her she was bringing over a client.

The owner of Nikita was stylish. I thought she was probably a lesbian. "People are tired of stupid drivers," she explained her business concept to me. "If a man has brains, then he has his own driver. That's not the case with women. A woman went to school, then had kids, then brought them up, then got a divorce, and she's close to thirty. She's smart, but who cares? Where can she find an outlet for her intelligence?"

I assured her that I would create all the conditions for my driver to apply her intelligence. They showed me some photos.

"We try not to use the photos," she explained, seeing my reaction. "Their charm is not in their looks."

I gave in to the sales pitch and agreed to give Alexandra a trial. "Get her a suit from Gaultier," Veronika said. "I saw one at Italmoda, with a crinkled shirt with a tie and wide trousers."

I hadn't seen Veronika since her return from Courchevel. She told me about her vacation the way you're supposed to talk about something that costs seventeen hundred dollars a night, not including the price of the lifts: with a touch of superciliousness, dropping names of movie stars and tycoons the way you drop pasta from the pot into the colander and from the colander onto the plate. The circumstances changed, but the contents remained the same: parties, affairs, furs, and that nasty Ksyusha (Ulyana, Svetlana, didn't matter) who looked marvelous . . .

Alexandra arrived at the house the next morning. I looked at her with curiosity: short hair, abrupt movements, and the odd habit of clicking her heels like a general's aide in the movies.

She had worked in a security job before. She was a sergeant.

"Do you have a gun permit?" I asked.

"Yes. Not for standard-issue weapons, of course."

We arrived at the police station. "If I'm not back in a half hour, call me from the car. If I don't answer, call this number, his name is Vadim, and tell him that I'm being held by the police."

I trusted them even less than I used to trust Oleg.

As I looked into Alexandra's face, I recalled her résumé, which showed that she had not had children or a divorce.

"You're not looking too good," said the cop, who six months earlier could not understand why I cared how my husband had died.

"I was in the hospital," I explained, not knowing why I bothered.

The other policeman, "our man" according to Vadim, came into the room, and I turned to him. "The killer is threatening my driver. I've set up bodyguards. But they call them—"

"We're not going to tap the phone," he interrupted. "There are no idiots left who call from their home number. Everyone watches TV."

Then he picked up the basin that was catching water from a leak in the ceiling and took it out to dump it. I waited for him. He came back and said, "Your Vova the Rat is hiding out. We've sent out an all-points bulletin on him. We can only wait—maybe he'll show up somewhere."

He switched on the electric kettle. The office seemed so homey that thoughts of Vova the Rat and broken fingers seemed unreal, or at any rate so far away as to be no threat whatsoever.

"Although I know stories," "our" cop said, lazily waving his arm. "We'll find him and the witness will run off just before the trial. Or during the trial. And once again, we'll be in the—"

He narrowed his eyes at me, apparently deciding whether he could use crude language. I was on their side, but the "once again" made me happy. They must land there fairly often, I thought meanly.

"But you'll still find Vova the Rat," I insisted, interrupting him.

It must be the genetic fear of the police that gives rise to the hope that if they often land in the word he didn't want to use, then if I get into trouble with them, they would end up there again.

"Where will we ever find law and order in our country?" I grumbled in the manner of Vladimir Pozner, the popular television host.

I asked Alexandra to drive me home, where I needed to have my injection. I dozed off in the car. I was still very weak.

Galya was without work. I wasn't allowed to have steam baths or massage after the kidney infection. I let her go home on a month's vacation, after exacting her promise to return. Her departure seemed like a catastrophe to me, but three days later I had forgotten all about her.

"Out of sight, out of mind." Stupid proverbs. I wondered how things were in London. That is, how Vanechka was.

Alexandra, hands in pockets, was kicking at the mounds of snow blocking my gate. I sat in the car and watched her. She seemed to be swearing. Not because she minded having to kick at the snow but because it fit the image she had of herself. She looked like an unfinished man. "I have to have a chat with her," I decided, and built a mental chain of logical moves that would persuade her to become more feminine. "If I had needed a man, I would have hired one instead of you," was going to be my starting point. "And when men want a woman, they want a creature that is absolutely the opposite of themselves: fragile, delicate—in a word, feminine."

"So, what is your sexual orientation?" I asked Alexandra when she got back in the car, tossing out her cigarette stub and filling the car with the smell of cheap tobacco. I was about to continue when she responded.

"Fifty-fifty," she replied, which was like knocking a chair out from under me. She looked at me in the rearview mirror expectantly.

Thank goodness the telephone rang. I told the bookkeeper that I would be in the office in a half hour.

"Can we collect all our debts and pay the bank a tranche of our loan?" I asked her, once I was seated at my desk. Now that half the staff was gone and the other looked at me with questioning sympathy, my office décor seemed excessively grand. It was as if I were wearing a Chanel ski suit and did not know how to ski. That actually did happen to me—when I thought twenty minutes would be long enough to master the sport.

"Here are the receipts. We've gathered up all the money. I paid the taxes yesterday—it's February already."

All right. I planned to organize the delivery campaign quickly. At the time that Boris ran off, I had everything in place. It wasn't huge money, but I would pay off my debts and give people work. I looked around my desk for the letters of intent signed with several warehouses.

I asked my secretary to hold all calls. I was not going to leave the office until I had solved all my problems.

But first I had to make one call. Recently, I had felt responsible for my driver's family. I worried whether he was taking his medication. He had to get well.

He answered the phone himself. He reported briefly, military style. "We didn't want to upset you," he explained at the end. "We thought you were still in the hospital."

I made him promise to tell me the minute anything else happened. I hung up and then dialed the protection agency. I tried to be calm, but I shouted at him anyway. It was easier to shout than to imagine what was going on in that apartment with the burned door.

"Their door was burned! You said your men were the best. Any idiot can knock out your guard. There's a sick man and an old woman in that place."

He weakly justified himself. The guard was overpowered by a man who came up the stairs with a dog. The guard thought he was a resident in the building and let him get too close. He set fire to the door. Following instructions, the other guard could not go outside the apartment to put out the fire. He stayed inside, protecting the clients. He called the police and they sent armed men. The neighbors called the firemen.

"It's just to scare them," he said. "No one got hurt, right? I'll increase the guards by two men at my expense. All right? For two days."

"For three," I said. "And pay for the repairs."

"Oh, no! My man was injured—he has a concussion."

The secretary peeked in and babbled something like, "Are you all right?" I motioned at her to go away.

Everything was very, very bad.

Vadim said the same thing. "He's trying to scare them off."

"Call the police. Can't they do anything? He's got to be somewhere, walking, eating, living?"

Vadim called. They promised to send his info to all railroad stations and airports. They swore even a mouse could not get through their net. I thought of the basin under the ceiling leak and was sure that the water was still dripping monotonously.

"Do you think I'm in danger?" I asked Vadim.

"I don't think so. But if you want, I can send you a bodyguard."

I sighed. "Basically, I have one. A girl. But without a gun."

"A girl?" Vadim snorted. "Buy her an OSA pistol. It's classified as non-lethal, but it shoots straight through a person at a couple of yards. It's like a gas pistol—but she'll need a permit."

"She's got one."

I had the contracts with the warehouses in my hands. I wanted to be Scarlett O'Hara and have the historical right to think about it tomorrow.

I went outside, feeling like a punching bag. I smoked real Dutch hash in the backseat, but Alexandra behaved as if I were munching an apple.

"Where to?" she asked cheerfully.

"The Gallery. Corner of Strastnoy and Trubnaya." I needed to be with people whose houses were not mortgaged and who themselves were probably the only ones who wanted to kill their drivers.

The first person I saw was Lena. Moscow is a huge city, but we all travel in our own vicious circles.

"My guy is away on business," she whispered so that everyone could hear her, "And we're partying."

"We're?" I asked.

They were living together now. After she left him, he left his wife. I had missed a lot while I was in the hospital.

I suggested we have a smoke. We each had a puff in the car. Alexandra had tactfully left the car.

"Who's that?" Lena asked.

"My driver."

"Cool."

At the table, waiting for us, were Katya, Tanya, and Kira with a lavender poodle. Lavender, because Kira was planning on wearing a lavender dress. But it was at the cleaner's. "It's not good to dye them too often," Kira explained the clash of her outfit with Blondie's fur.

Lena and I were boisterous in our sympathies. Even after the topic of conversation had changed.

"Are you two stoned?" Katya asked. The three of us headed to the toilets, where we sprayed the air with three different perfumes and then lit up.

Kira was listening intently to Tanya. "My gynecologist says, 'Let me sew you up, you'll be like a little girl again.' Naturally, I didn't sew it all up."

"Of course not," Lena interrupted, grinning. "You're no fool."

"But I did sew it up a bit. I felt like a schoolgirl, you wouldn't believe it. My bum came home late. I hadn't told him anything, I figured I'd surprise him—with new sensations. But he was completely drunk. So we get into bed and do you know what he did?" She made a tragic pause.

"What?" we chorused.

"He was so drunk he thought he had deflowered somebody. He embraced me and begged forgiveness. He kept promising me presents until he fell asleep."

We laughed until our stomachs ached and we couldn't breathe, but we couldn't stop.

"It's not funny," Tanya said.

"That's for sure," I managed to squeeze out.

The waiter came over. We hid our laughing faces behind the menus and waved our hands at him that we weren't ready yet.

"Later," Lena said, choking, doubled over with laughter.

"No. Bring me spring rolls," Tanya ordered, as if we weren't with her.

"For us, too," Kira said, meaning herself and Blondie.

When we quieted down a bit, I ordered steamed cabbage. I had to stick to a limited diet for a month. That's why I wasn't drinking wine.

We had another joint and went to First. In the middle of the floor, surrounded by his bodyguards, Katya's tycoon was dancing. The bodyguards were dancing, too, but not even pretending to enjoy it.

"I need a smoke," Katya said, and we headed for the bathroom, this time with Kira and Blondie.

"You're not going to be all stressed that he's here?" I asked in the cramped toilet stall.

"Do you want to go to Cabaret instead?" Lena offered.

"I can't stand Cabaret," Kira said.

"Doesn't matter." Katya took a deep lungful of smoke and held it for a long time.

"Maybe he won't notice us," Kira suggested, taking the joint from Katya.

"You wish," Lena said. "He always notices everything. He's always working."

"Nice work." I flushed just in case. "Dancing."

"You sound like my mother. She works till six and if they ask her to stay twenty minutes longer, she's indignant for several days. His workday is twenty-four hours. But if he came home and said 'I'm tired,' my mother would ask, 'It's not like you've been hauling logs, is it?' "

"Look, she's defending him," Kira said.

"Let's all feel sorry for him," Lena suggested.

"Maybe we can chip in for a present?" I suggested.

"Or just give him some money," Katya replied.

We filed out of the toilet stall with maximally neutral expressions. Two girls exchanged a meaningful look behind our backs.

Some friends were drinking champagne at the first semicircular table we came to, and we joined them shamelessly. One of them was paying a lot of attention to Kira. He called her Malvina, after the lovely character from a children's book. We burst out laughing every time he spoke, sometimes even drowning out the music. The tenth time he called her Malvina and Blondie Artemon, the name of Malvina's little black dog, I pulled Katya away from the table. We went back into the bathroom, rolled another joint, and then I called Alexandra.

"I'm going to call you Alex. Do you mind?" I asked over the loud music.

She didn't. I asked her to bring the spray can of Salamander black shoe dye from the trunk of the car.

Back at the table, we asked Kira if we could hold her dog. She gave us Blondie and went off to dance. Blondie kept wriggling and did not want to be sprayed with Salamander. But we were determined to turn her into Artemon.

Only her left paw was still lavender when she got away from us. She ran along the table toward the dance floor. We tried to catch her, knocking down glasses and spilling champagne on ourselves. She jumped down on the floor.

"Get her!" I shouted, pushing aside everyone in my path.

"Get the dog!" shouted Katya in the heat of pursuit.

Katya's tycoon caught the dog.

"Artemon," I said happily.

"Blondie?" cried a horrified Kira.

"Hi," Katya said, looking at her tycoon's stained hands.

We drank champagne at his table, and I forgot all about my diet.

"I love your haircut." He touched Katya's buzz cut. She tried not to talk so that he wouldn't realize what we had been doing in the bathroom.

He tried to get her to talk. She kept silent. That took half the night.

He had his bodyguards take her home. Tanya, Kira, and Artemon had already left.

I got in Lena's car and we followed Alexandra in mine. I called my driver before we got to the checkpoint on the Ring Road.

"Yes." Alexandra said sternly.

"If you see cops, start weaving. Lena's been drinking."

Before the checkpoint, she swung from side to side along the road so hard that the highway cops rushed out at her as if on wings, blowing their whistles and waving their sticks.

"What should I do?" Lena asked, watching the hullabaloo.

"Drive calmly. Pay no attention to anyone."

We said good-bye around Barvikha, and I switched to my own car.

"I'm going to call you Alex," I reminded my driver.

"Look at this fool. She's wearing a dress from the Vivienne Westwood collection of two seasons ago."

20.

I lay in bed and thought how the entire two-room apartment of my child-hood would have fit in my thirty-square-meter bedroom—including the kitchen and combined bathroom and toilet. I mentally sketched the walls, making space for the storeroom and closet (I didn't remember if we had any), and I came up with a very spacious house for Barbie. I filled it with two children (I had a brother), mother, and father. It was fine if you were the child. Then I imagined myself as the mother—not so much to clean, and then as the father—and went off to the football game. That did not exhaust my need to fantasize, so I tried to imagine myself as their dog. In the house for Barbie, two rooms with a kitchen and bathroom, in my bedroom. I couldn't. I couldn't imagine myself as the cat, either. I decided that smoking dope had a bad effect on the imagination.

I went downstairs. Everything was orderly and tea was served in the dining room.

"Will you have breakfast?" Alex asked in a kindly tone. She was on the couch, leafing through a glossy magazine.

"Have you seen the Filipina?" I wondered.

Alex nodded. Apparently, the Filipina was invisible only to me.

I ate in total silence and went off to work with Alex at the wheel. After last night's nondietetic evening, my kidneys did not hurt, which led me to believe that I was absolutely healthy. But just in case, I doubled my dose of pills.

Nothing was working. My idea for the delivery company was falling apart at the seams, like a woman's shirt on a body builder. The warehouses I had hoped to work with had found other partners. The stores had broken their contracts with me.

I felt like a little girl who had wanted to put on lipstick and ended up smearing her face. I rocked back on the legs of my plush fuzzy armchair, and my apathy was turning me into plush. My fuzzy brains had curled up in my head and gone to sleep.

My entire body, from fuzzy brains to pedicure, was imbued with profound indifference. The workday was over and I was all alone in the office.

Like an exhibitionist enjoying her nakedness, I was enjoying my sorrow. It was wrong, but pleasant. I thought that I was sleeping with open eyes. I was afraid to move because I knew that the smallest movement would break the spell.

I wanted to get through this day, and I believed that tomorrow everything would work out.

There was a knock at the door. I kept forgetting about Alex. She brought me the phone: Serge's driver was calling. And she turned on the light.

His mother was having a hypertensive crisis, a blood-pressure spike. She needed to be in the hospital. Their car had been burned to a crisp. Could I send a driver?

No, I couldn't. It was too dangerous. She had to stay home.

"You must understand," I begged of the sick, frightened man. "They may be watching your apartment. We can't take that risk. I'll send a doctor to you. He will stay with her as long as she needs it."

He said nothing. It would have been better if he had shouted and sent me and all the Rats to Hell.

He said nothing. I wanted to be next to him, to support him in this exhausting battle for principles and peace. Or, maybe, I wanted him to support me.

I called my doctor. He promised to do everything he could.

Alex was in the office during all these calls.

"Poor girl," I thought. "Just two days working for me and you've had to deal with drugs, tricking the highway police, a sick old lady who might be killed, and me, hanging around the office for hours."

"Have you eaten?" I asked.

"Yes, with the others." She waved in the direction of the reception area.

"Wait for me. We'll leave soon."

I decided to go to Veronika's, to tuck my feet under me in a big armchair in her dark, curtained study and hide from the world. Maybe even have a cry together. But then, like the bonus bunny in a pinball game, Igor popped up. Of course, he'd be home by now.

Then I would go to Lena's. Sit by the fireplace, stare at the flickering flames, and sip red wine from oversized goblets. We'd talk about men, how they were all shit. And life, too. Only the wine and the fire made sense.

From her "hello" I could tell that she was not alone. Of course, I forgot about her boyfriend. It's so inconvenient when a man appears in your girlfriend's life. If I went there I would feel like an actor coming out onstage without having read the play.

I hung up without a word. The prospect of cuddling up in the soft pillows of Katya's Provazi in front of the television set seemed attractive. Her rational mind would quickly set out my problems like an equation, into its component parts. She would multiply, divide, find the square root, and determine the percentage. Then she'd find pi and convince me that all the questions have been solved.

She was heading for a party given by DON-Stroy with her tycoon. They had reunited thanks to Kira's little dog. "He gave me only ninety minutes to get ready," she fumed, her voice trembling with excitement. "What do you think he wants from me?"

"Love," I replied. "Once they've conquered all the countries possible, generals come home." I did not tell her that this happens to them because they're undisciplined. The richer the man and the higher his position, the more undisciplined he allows himself to be. Very few manage to find a linch-pin that helps them avoid it. They lean on it throughout their lives. Usually it's family. House, wife, children, dog. Computer, mother-in-law, sports channel.

I felt abandoned. The roads of all humanity seemed to lead south while mine led north. I couldn't see why it had happened to me.

"Because you are strong," Vanechka explained. I'd called him in London. "You would be a prime minister here."

I often heard that. When others were pitied, I heard: you're strong. When others drank white wine and listened to words of love, I had to think about saving my driver. And his mother. And giving their life back to them.

While my girlfriends enjoyed love, I had to keep killing someone. I was moving into the ranks of serial killers.

Oleg's phone was on voicemail. I asked him to get back to me urgently.

I didn't feel like going home. In the quiet of my rooms, the decision I just made would chase me from corner to corner and not let me sleep.

Alex was happy for the change in plan. She drove carefully through the Moscow night, pushing the radio buttons every minute. No sooner would I like a song than she would switch to another station. I said nothing, silently fighting my growing irritation.

DON-Stroy Construction was having another of its huge blasts. Their entertainment budget was probably equal to their construction-material budget.

I didn't have an invitation, so I asked Katya to meet me outside. We sat at her tycoon's table with some of his friends, most of whom were already working for him and the rest were dreaming about it. People kept coming over to greet him respectfully. Girls at neighboring tables looked enviously at Katya and me, and we bathed in the waves of his majesty.

"You were looking for me?" Oleg whispered in my ear, suddenly appearing behind me. He shook hands in a dignified manner with all the men at our table, and complimented Katya on her new haircut.

"I didn't expect to see you here," I said honestly, after we had moved away from the table.

He shrugged vaguely. "I was sure I'd see you here."

Now I shrugged. Offhandedly. "I want to kill Vova the Rat."

Our shoulders were moving as much as they would in the Jewish folk dance to "Hava Nagilah."

His response was an indifferent shrug.

"Will you help me?" I persisted.

"I can't." He shook his head, and I saw sincere regret in his eyes. "I can't be involved in something like that now."

"Why not?"

His shoulders swayed mysteriously. "Because . . . Is it urgent?"

"It is." I nodded like a telegraph clerk receiving a telegram.

"I can't."

The bank's announcement of the repossession of my property was already on the repo people's desk. They sent me a statement. Asking me to sign. Apparently, I needed to go pack up.

My house, worth $3.5 million, was being sold to pay the bank loan of $120,000. How incredibly stupid. I had to call Vadim and borrow the money.

But how would I pay it back? And what if he refused? How humiliating that refusal would be.

I thought about my director, Boris. A bug that was not squashed in time had laid eggs because I was too lazy to move my foot. And now they would devour the entire garden. I wasn't angry with him. I only felt dispassionate disdain.

Veronika's husband, Igor, had that kind of money. I pictured myself coming to him for a loan and he would look at me mockingly, his feet on his desk. I'd rather sell the house.

There was Katya's tycoon. He must get several such requests a day.

There was Vanechka, who probably, as a Brit, could not imagine lending that much money.

There were my diamonds. But who would buy them?

Borrowing money meant admitting my business failure. Boris's treachery was also a failure. I should not have created a situation in which one person was supposed to solve all the questions.

I walked from room to room, and my Filipina avoided me with enviable persistence.

If only Serge were alive. I was so tired of having to make decisions. With him, I could play ostrich and bury my head in the sand. He would have handled the collateral issue.

If Serge were alive, he would be holding his son and looking at Svetlana with warm, grateful eyes. What if, in fact, he had loved her?

As soon as I was dressed, the Filipina was at the front door, seeing me off with a polite smile. Her dress with its long apron from Majordomo made her look like a heroine of some Mexican soap opera.

I had not warned Svetlana that I was coming. I realized that I should have bought a toy for the baby. Svetlana was disheveled and I doubted she had washed. The child was screaming in Masha's crib.

"Could you sit with Little Serge for a few hours?" Her eyes beseeched me.

"Why?" I was frightened by that prospect.

"He's got a runny nose, I can't take him outside." She was on the verge of tears. I couldn't understand why she wasn't soothing the baby.

"Do you need to buy something?"

"No." Her eyes filled with tears. "I'm tired. I'm buried inside these four walls." She looked around like a badgered animal.

"Calm the baby," I said.

"I won't." She was screeching now and threw herself on the unmade bed and pounded her fists on the pillows. "Let him scream. I don't care! He cries day and night."

I picked him up. His tiny body reminded me of a good-quality doll. "Hush, little guy," I whispered to him, while my hands remembered how to hold a baby. "It's all right, it's all right."

As I mumbled to him, I paced the room. The baby quieted down and cuddled his head trustingly on my shoulder. "Look how upset Mama is. She's so pretty. Get ready." The last was for Svetlana.

"Where are we going?" she said through her tears. The blanket was on the floor, her hair was tangled, her eyes puffy.

"We're going to go meet the grandparents," I said, surprising myself.

Svetlana gasped and stared at me suspiciously.

"Come on, come on. Just pull yourself together first."

That took a half hour.

"Wasn't your mother helping?" I asked Svetlana when she got into the backseat with the baby in a carrier.

"She's staying with my brother. The crying made her blood pressure shoot up."

She kept fussing with the baby. I wanted to say, Don't worry, they'll like him. But I kept quiet.

My mother-in-law opened the door. She clasped her hands happily when she saw me. "How are you?" I asked tenderly.

"Oh," she said, waving off the question. A tear glistened on her face, but she turned away. "And who's this pretty little baby?"

While Svetlana unbundled Little Serge, I led my mother-in-law into the kitchen. Her husband was watching TV in there. He jumped up when he saw me.

"Look who's here."

I shut the door behind me. My mother-in-law gave me a quizzical look. It felt as if I had lived my entire life for the sake of this moment. I would tell them that they had Little Serge and then die. "That is your grandson. His name is Serge." I don't know if I managed a smile.

Serge's father kept kissing the baby and Svetlana in turn. His mother sat on the couch with me, holding my hand, and letting tears of joy course down her cheeks.

"Upsy-daisy!" the grandfather shouted, lifting the baby up to the ceiling.

"Thank you," whispered my mother-in-law, patting my hair.

I managed a smile. They had a lot to talk about with Svetlana. I left, saying I had things to do.

Lena was gabbing on the phone. She opened the door to let me in without stopping her monologue.

"They have chess and other games, an astrologist comes once a week, beautician on Tuesdays, dance lessons on Thursdays, and Wednesdays there's Brazilian cooking. Saturday night is literary, they read poetry . . . and there's exercise class . . ."

"Is that some day care center?" I asked, walking through to the living room.

"Listen, I'll call you back, but think about it. They drink tea and gossip there. It's a civilized version of the bench in front of the building. You buy a year's membership and you're in. So long, give it some thought."

After she hung up, she explained to me. "Katya's affair with the tycoon is getting serious, and her mother's not very happy about it. So I suggested organizing a club for parents. We'll all chip in. My mother doesn't have any-thing to do, either. They can meet there and pay less attention to our lives."

"Great," I said, thinking that my mother would go, too. "So Katya's hav-ing a real affair?"

"Yes, she's moving in with him."

Judging by all the men's clothing scattered about, someone had moved in with Lena. She followed my glance. "We're thinking about getting mar-ried," she announced triumphantly.

"Great," I said again. If I told her my house was being repossessed, Lena would feel sorry for me. I'd feel better. Maybe we'd even have a cry to-gether. But that would mean that Katya would hear about it. And Kira. Then Tanya. Then all of Rublyovka. I would walk around and think, "They're all looking at me and pitying the failed businesswoman."

Silently, I picked out a CD. I chose Pink.

"We'll have to build a new house. He has nothing left, his wife got everything. She's such a shark. Good thing she left him the car."

"Has he proposed?"

"No, but he asked if I didn't mind."

"And you said?"

"I said I'd think about it. Can you imagine? He doesn't eat breakfast. What luck for me."

She moved to the music, smoothly, like a cat. "We'll have the wedding at the Metropole. I want to give him something extraordinary. Any ideas?"

I shrugged. "Usually it's the groom who gives presents."

"So what? I'll give him something, too," she said with a stubborn shake of the head. "You know, he doesn't want me to accept money from my ex."

"Great."

"Is that the only word you know? Great, great . . ."

The phone rang.

"Hello," Lena said coyly. But she changed her tone instantly to a pa-tronizing one. "Your daddy? Wouldn't you like to say hello to me first?"

A few seconds later, she wasn't quite so friendly. "No, not until you say hello to me. She hung up. The nerve. That's his daughter. She's twelve," Lena explained.

The phone rang again. "Hello. No, I told you, not until you say hello . . . She hung up again. He must have his mobile switched off."

"Why bother? Just say he's not here," I came to the girl's defense. "She's just a kid."

"A kid?" Lena was indignant. "I could hear her mother breathing on the extension. She's making her call him. She said, 'I'm not talking to you, give me my father.'"

The phone rang again. Lena shouted, "Hello!"

Her face changed, tears filled her eyes. She nodded obediently but then started shouting again. "I will not tolerate your daughter's rudeness. I didn't shout at her, she's lying. And you're yelling at me. Don't you dare yell!" Lena threw down the phone and started bawling. "I'm sick of it. Sick and tired. I have to fight for everything. Even for respect. Remember how he didn't say hello at the restaurant?" Her eyes were burning like headlights on a dark road. "If a man behaves like that once, that means he'll shout at you and humiliate you whenever he wants."

I was about to tell her that my house was being repossessed when the phone rang again. "Please take it," Lena asked. "It's him. Tell him I'm crying and don't want to talk to him."

It was Katya. She invited us over to her place for a family dinner. Lena took a long time dressing and I put on makeup at the mirror. You don't dine with tycoons every day.

Katya's sixty-year-old mother, who tried to look younger, met us in jeans with huge letters of Svarovski crystals on her rear end spelling out RICH. "Did you see yourselves in the latest issue of *Vogue*?" she demanded critically.

The social-life column showed Katya and Lena with their arms around each other at a Moët & Chandon event smiling into the camera. The caption read: "Social Lionesses."

"I think it's pretty good," Lena said in a satisfied tone.

"I think what's pretty good is when they print your name and what you do," fumed Katya's mother.

But Katya was happy. "Look at this fool," she said, handing me the magazine open to a photo of a girl for whom a friend of ours was recently left by her husband. "She's wearing a dress from the Vivienne Westwood collection of two seasons ago. I had one like it then."

"Then I got it," Katya's mother said with feigned humility. "I get the hand-me-downs."

I squinted at her six-hundred-dollar jeans and sympathy stuck in my craw.

We went through the society pages in the new *Vogue*. "Rustam's got a new cookie," Lena commented, looking over the page for familiar faces.

"What's the fur on Kurbatskaya?" Katya was leaning over the page so closely I wanted to offer her a jeweler's loupe.

"Marusya designed it for her. Look, Ulyana's tits are going to fall right off the page." Lena started chuckling. "It could be an advertising campaign. You open the magazine, and Ulyana's tits fall out—right into your lap."

Dinner with Katya's tycoon was a success. We were charmed by his quick mind and casual manner. The friendly atmosphere was disrupted only once thanks to Katya's mother. "Is that your girlfriend? Ex?" she asked with artificial simplicity, pointing at the television screen. The star of the latest Russian soap opera was the actress who had ruined Katya's life many years ago, when the tycoon had left her the first time.

"Don't be silly, I've always had only one girl—your daughter," he said with a broad smile.

I thought about how much more interesting it must be for tycoons to be with movie stars. Actresses have the same overly high opinion of themselves, and to make an impression on them, tycoons have to try a little harder than with us simple girls from the Rublyovo-Uspenskoe Highway.

Katya watched her mother and calculated how much it would cost her for the parents' club. It really was a good idea. It just had to be made clear that it wasn't a nursing home.

"You know," Lena said to me on the phone as we rehashed the dinner, "my mother once said to me, when I gave her a pair of earrings for her birthday: 'How pretty. But if you hadn't told me there were diamonds in them, I would never have seen them on my own.'"

"That's why they're our mothers," I said, defending the woman who hated small diamonds.

"Yes, I know," Lena sighed. "But sometimes you just want to hear a 'thank you.'"

Someone called twice and hung up. I was cleaning up Masha's room. The nanny was sick, so I had to stay home. I went through Masha's toys, notebooks, albums, purses, hair bands, pads, and books. I dispatched half right into the plastic garbage bag. Children never part with things on their own.

How would she part with this house?

I tried to be abstract about it: I couldn't believe that I would lose this house, that this would not be my yard, not be my rooms, not be my address. It felt like someone wanted to borrow my car. Just for the day. Of course, you're worried. What if they get into a fender bender or it's carjacked? But it's just for a day. And then everything will be fine again.

The phone rang again, and someone hung up right after I said hello.

Who could it be? What if it were Vova the Rat?

Fear is when you don't care how you look. It's when your hands sweat. Fear is when you need only one thing: to screen yourself off from danger. And you're ready to use anything or anyone for that screen. At the very first second. That's the second when betrayals happen. Because after that moment you break something inside yourself with a crunch and then you're in shape to think properly.

Vova the Rat did not need me. Unless he was a schizophrenic idiot or maniac killer.

I called Vadim. "Are they planning to catch that Vova?" I asked in irritation. "I'm worried about the driver's family. They've already had their car burned."

"I have one more lever to use. I'll try to juice them up a bit," Vadim promised.

"Or else the family will move in with them at the precinct," I promised.

"You need to relax," deduced my husband's friend.

God, don't take away my house!

That made it sound as if the stupid bank were God.

God, give me the strength to get through this.

No, that wasn't right either. Everyone bears the cross that he can. I'd rather not have the strength for it.

God, perform a miracle!

Kira's husband left
her for another.
Strangely, she didn't
dye Blondie black.

21.

The summer collections were in the stores. Spring was in the air. Everyone went on a diet and exercised. I was in the café of World Class Health Club in Zhukovka, deciding where to go. To the left was the spa, to the right, the gym. I decided to start my new health program with the pool.

That's where Tanya was starting hers. She was sitting on the edge and thinking about how to make her husband have a church wedding. Her idea was that after a religious ceremony he would never leave her.

"Should I tell him that the priest at church scolds me for living in sin?" she asked as I swam by, intent on the regularity of my breathing.

"Yes," I said, fitting the word in one breath.

"Or maybe, I should tell him that our children will pay for our sins? That's true, isn't it?" she continued when I came by on my fourth lap.

"Not bad." I was still keeping the rhythm, but I was getting tired.

"Or, maybe I should buy a wedding gown for ten thousand dollars or so—we couldn't just throw it away. We'd have to have a church wedding."

"I think that if he realizes he's getting married because you spent money, the whole idea will lose its higher meaning." I decided to catch my breath before continuing my swim.

Tanya deftly lowered herself into the water. She flipped onto her back and floated, barely moving her legs.

"I'm off," I said.

"Did you have a good workout?" Alex asked in the car.

"Terrific," I muttered, through gritted teeth.

Katya greeted me with open arms. "I'm afraid to jinx it," she said with a glorious smile, "but we're in love. And he wants children."

"And I want food. I've come from the gym."

"I'm impressed." There was respect in her voice. "I'm not allowed right now. I'm trying to get pregnant. I've bought about twenty tests, so I don't have to run out for them later."

Katya's housekeeper fed us scalloped potatoes. I had come to appreciate simple food with my Filipina's cooking.

"After sex I have to lie on my back with my legs up," Katya explained, "and basically we can only do it when the doctor says so: they do an ultrasound for fertility peaks. It's not very romantic," she grumbled, "but I think he had enough romance before me."

I began wondering if it was safe for me to swim with my kidney infection.

"You wouldn't have a hundred twenty thou handy, would you?" I asked Katya over dessert.

"In dollars?"

I nodded.

"No, I don't."

"I'm sorry."

"So am I, to tell the truth. But I think that will change soon."

We had a wafer torte for dessert.

Oleg's classmate was killed in a plane crash. The pilot died, too. The private plane crashed ten minutes after takeoff.

There was a time when I did not trust Oleg. I used to leave my jewelry in the car when I went to meet him. Why did I decide that he would change when he stopped being poor? There is always money around that does not belong to you. For the time being.

What had he said? "I can't get involved in anything like this now."

I called him. Voice mail.

"Oleg, I wanted to express my condolences. And thank God that you weren't flying with him. Bye."

If only I could lock myself in the house. With my books and TV. Have a moat. And allow someone to cross the moat with fresh caviar for lunch. Pretty soon there wouldn't be any place to bring it. The bank was taking the house.

Katya was given a Porsche Cayenne SUV on March Eighth for Women's Day (a cross between Valentine's Day and Mother's Day). She was expecting flowers from Van Cleef. For her ears and finger.

Following her usual pattern, Lena broke up with her fiancé. And gave up all hope of getting married. Now, when she described a woman, she simply stated how many years she had been married. For instance: "There's Olya. Look at her skirt. She's been married nine years. She has two children." That meant that she liked the skirt.

Veronika's husband came home at nine in the morning. They were supposed to have left for the airport at seven that morning. They were going to Egypt to scuba dive. At 8:30, Veronika had the housekeeper unpack and sent the children back to bed.

Tanya still hadn't come up with a way to make her husband go through a church ceremony. Her latest plan was to go to the hospital, claim to be near death and that only a church wedding would help. We refused even to discuss that version.

Kira's husband left her for another. Strangely, she didn't dye Blondie black. They had been married for eleven years. And all those years he had put up with Kira's lovers as meekly as he did her dogs. Until he found the strength to fall in love with someone else.

We were in the glass-enclosed veranda of Mario, eating pasta with white truffles (at thirty dollars a gram), and drinking martinis on ice from glasses that looked like upside-down ballet tutus.

"I could hire someone to break her legs," Kira proposed, after her fourth martini.

"Look. It's Iskander. They say he divorced his wife." Tanya quickly pulled out her compact and freshened her lipstick.

"But he wasn't in *Harper's Bazaar*'s list of the ten most eligible bachelors in Moscow," Lena said confidently.

"He gave his page to Sorkin," Katya informed us.

"He doesn't need it," I sighed. "He could marry anyone in this restaurant and in this city. Not even marry them."

"Right," Kira said belligerently.

"You bet it's right. If a convertible Bentley wrapped in pink ribbons were delivered to your front door, would you resist? He can easily do that. And if you resist, he'll buy you a house in Marbella the next day. And then what?"

Kira sighed dreamily. I could tell that she would accept.

"Every woman wants that," I said. "You almost feel sorry for him. Can you imagine what a drag it is for him to deal with us women?"

"Girls, let's teach that bitch a lesson," Kira returned us to real life.

"How?" Lena asked.

"We could give her a scare," Katya suggested.

"You could throw acid in her face," Tanya said.

"No, then she'll know it's me," Kira countered.

"Let her guess." Veronika ordered another round of martinis. "The point is for her to leave him alone."

"Girls," Lena said, looking around. "Let's not get together more than three at a time—all the men are avoiding us. We're too much. No one's sending champagne over or anything."

"We should go to New York," Lena said. "Have you seen *Sex and the City?*"

"Yes, that's in New York," Kira sighed. "Here it's No Sex in the City. We should make a series, starring everyone in this place."

"Do you remember fifteen years ago?" Tanya shut her eyes dreamily.

"There was sex fifteen years ago," Lena said firmly.

"But no money," Katya noted.

"Whom can I ask to call her and give her a scare?" Kira ordered a tiramisu. Mario has the best tiramisu in Moscow. And the best atmosphere.

"I'll ask Borisych." Veronika started looking for her phone, but couldn't find it in all her pockets. Lena offered hers. Veronika starting rummaging through Lena's bag. "Oh!" she exclaimed and froze. "This is so exciting. Condoms in your bag. A long-forgotten sensation."

"Better look for the phone instead," Kira hurried her.

"Hello. Borisych. Listen, my dear. If you don't want Igor to learn that I didn't get to that meeting because you were drunk, do this favor for my friend."

She explained the situation. She asked him to be very scary. "Well, for instance, what will you say?" She was giving him a little quiz. She made a face and moved the phone away from her ear. "You are so rude, Borisych. No, no, that's fine. And as soon as you make the call, let me know."

We ordered another round.

"I'm selling the house," I said.

"You're kidding," Veronika replied.

"I'm tired of living in Rublyovka." It's not how I wanted to sound, so I changed my tone from arrogant to lazy. "All those traffic jams. Putin isn't going to move, you know. Plus, I was offered a very good price."

"How much?" Kira asked.

"Three and a half."

"I wouldn't sell for anything," Tanya said.

"Me, neither," Katya sighed.

"I look at it as nothing more than real estate—if they're giving good money, I'll sell and buy another."

"But it should be in Rublyovka, too," Tanya said. "You'll never be able to live anywhere else, you know."

Borisych called back. He said that she heard him out in silence and hung up.

"That's all right. She'll think twice before stealing people's husbands," Kira threatened.

"What a fool," Tanya said, and laughed.

I wondered if this would be as funny tomorrow morning.

Lena's phone rang. "It's my guy," she said, looking at the ID. "Maybe I shouldn't pick up? The hell with him . . . Let him call his wife."

She answered, chin held high. "Hello. Of course I'm not home. I was called in for emergency surgery. Didn't I tell you I've become a surgeon?"

In the doorway, I bumped into Oleg. He was coming in, surrounded by bodyguards. "What a gorgeous hunk!" I said sarcastically.

"Who is that?" Katya asked.

"I think he's got a nickel company or some factory in Ukraine. Nothing less than that, I'm sure," I replied.

Oleg smiled at me as at an old friend.

I waved prettily.

"We're selling the house," I told Masha at dinner.

"Why?" She looked up in surprise.

"It needs to be done."

"Hurrah!" she said, throwing her napkin in the air.

"Why are you so happy?" It was my turn to be surprised.

"That means we'll leave here and I won't have to ride to school with Nikita every day."

"I didn't know that was a problem for you."

Masha said nothing. Then: "Our teacher told us that if something bad happens, you have to find a silver lining." Masha looked at me attentively.

"And what makes you think that selling the house is a bad thing?"

I put more cabbage slaw on my plate and offered some to my daughter. She refused.

"Because your eyes are sad." Her plate was untouched. Masha was still too young to be able to eat and talk about serious things.

"But don't worry," she whispered. "Everything will be all right. I asked Santa Claus. Not for that real porcelain tea service for Barbie, but for things to be good. And for us to be healthy."

I hadn't known about the tea set. I got her a new tape player from Santa. That's what I thought she had wanted.

"You didn't say anything to me." I couldn't even imagine that Masha would ask Santa for the tea set and he wouldn't give it to her.

"I saw it at Winnie. But I told myself not to think about it. I knew what I would ask from Santa."

"Would you like me to buy it for you for March 8th?"

Masha's eyes sparkled. "The full set or just for tea?"

I pretended to think about it. "Well, I think the full set."

"Hurrah!" Masha shouted again. "I told you everything would be fine. There's also a real table lamp," she recalled, "so teensy tiny."

"I'm sure there are lots of things there," I said with a smile.

I had taken Masha to school. The sun blazed through the huge living room windows. It was the first day of spring.

There's something crazy about people welcoming the first snow and the first day of spring with the same enthusiasm. They must be happy that life is not standing still. Even though we all know where life is moving.

I played rap through the powerful speakers.

Hey, Filipina, where are you hiding?

I danced with the rays of sunshine, then with my reflection in the windows, then with the drums, then with the vocalist's voice. Then I danced by myself, not needing a partner.

I felt absolutely free. I was alone in an enormous, empty house. I could jump on the couches. Which I did. I could take off my T-shirt and dance topless.

No, somewhere in the house, she was . . . Nonsense! I took off my T-shirt and waved it about, like a pop star onstage.

Thank you very much, dear Filipina, for this intoxicating feeling, when no one is watching you, bumbling underfoot, spreading out basins and mops, or pestering you with recipes.

I turned down the music and went to take a bath. There were three messages on the phone machine. All from my doctor.

"I've been calling all morning."

"The music was up too high."

He said that the driver's mother needed to be hospitalized. The blood pressure crisis was over, but she needed the right rehab treatment in the hospital. Or he couldn't be held responsible.

"Thank you," I said.

In the spring, it's even easier to make decisions. It must be the light. When it's that light, it's not scary. Lying in my tub, you can look at the trees. God, how I didn't want to leave.

That Vova should not be allowed to walk this earth. He should not look at trees. Trees were for the select few. I hated him.

I hate it when the phone rings while I'm in the tub. Veronika. Igor had a huge fight with her. Kira's husband had called him.

"Can you imagine," sobbed Veronika, "that idiot Tanya told her husband everything. She said, 'You see how good I am, I put up with everything from you. Some people hire bandits and plan to throw acid in girl's faces.'"

"And he called Kira's husband," I guessed. "Male solidarity?"

"Of course. And he called mine. He was furious. But I won't tell on Borisych—he'll still come in handy."

"What an idiot," I said, agreeing with Veronika.

Alex, I thought. *Alex can kill Vova. She has such a powerful face. For money.*

Or, my driver's brother. He's a mercenary creature. No, he'd start blackmailing me.

Alex had the OSA handgun. I bought it for her. It can go through a person at ten feet. She could pretend it was self-defense.

As I shampooed my hair, I admitted to myself that Alex wouldn't kill anyone.

What an important role Oleg turned out to have played in my life. I was helpless without him.

"What if I want to have someone killed, what should I do?" I asked Katya when she called to talk over Tanya's stupidity.

"You should go see a psychiatrist," Katya said. "Is this because of Tanya?"

"No I'm annoyed by the president of America." What was I saying?

"Oh." Katya paused. "I am, too, to be honest."

She could not become pregnant on her own. Katya decided to do it in vitro, a test tube baby. "It's a horrible process," she told me. "You have to see the doctor every other day—I go to Torganova, she's the best. Every day you have to have shots in the belly, and besides that you have endless shots in the ass, until something happens with the corpus luteum. I wanted to hire a surrogate mother," Katya said with a sigh, "so that she would do all these things. You know, there are lots of women willing to do it—and it only costs ten thousand dollars plus renting an apartment for her somewhere and assigning a bodyguard. And you bring her fruit and books. And classical music. Convenient, no? But he wouldn't agree to it. Very stubborn about it. He said, 'I don't want my child to have genes from some unknown collective farm worker.' Even though it's been proven long ago that nothing is passed through the mother's blood. But you can't make him understand that."

Katya sighed deeply.

"Don't worry." I tried to be consoling. "You'll have this great belly. And there will be a baby inside. Which do you want?"

"I don't know. A girl probably. You can dress her up."

"A boy is good, too. What does he want?"

"He doesn't care, he just wants a child. You can imagine how much, since he went to have his sperm tested."

"How is that done?"

"I laughed so hard. We went to this office, all these pregnant women waiting, photographs of children everywhere. I had promised that no one would even notice him, but he's got his bodyguards with him, see? Everyone's watching him. I gave him a key and pointed to the door—that's where you go. I thought he would kill me on the spot. But instead he grinned and pulled me in with him. It's a tiny room with a copy of *Playboy* on the chair. Then you come out with a test tube and everybody stares at you again. No privacy."

"And?"

"We're waiting for the results. A lot depends on the mobility of those spermatozoa."

I dropped by Winnie. The collector's porcelain service for Barbie cost just a little less than my formal Meissen. I looked at the one-inch table lamps, too. With real silk shades and electric cords. I bought one.

Barbie maintenance was more expensive than baby maintenance.

In the newborn department I bought a few pairs of pants and an outfit for Little Serge. I hoped that Svetlana had gotten a grip. Before she had him, she had talked about her "big plans." That's all they're good for: talk. The poor baby had been hiccupping from crying.

Svetlana told me that she wanted to move in with Serge's parents and asked for help with the move. Of course, I would help.

It was getting close to the anniversary of Serge's murder. His friends would gather. Svetlana and I would sit next to his parents. Next to us, our children. I wouldn't go at all. Or . . . I'd have everyone in a restaurant, and not invite Svetlana.

My mother-in-law was excited by the prospect of their grandson living with them. I watched their happy faces as they bustled about and decided that my anxieties over Svetlana were caused by the usual female jealousy. Little Serge had to have been born if only to reanimate these old people, who were dried up from weeping.

"You see how things are," Serge's mother said, almost apologetically.

I nodded.

"Yes . . . She needs to get married, she's so young."

I gave my mother-in-law a surprised look. She replied with the wise gaze of a seventy-year-old woman. "We'll bring up Little Serge. Our grand-son." A tender smile spread over her face. "Oh, yes, we bought Masha a doll for March 8th. Please give it to her for us."

I wouldn't have been offended if they had forgotten. Happiness frees people of obligations.

"As soon as I figure out how to explain all this to Masha . . . Little Serge . . . I'll bring her here."

My mother-in-law smiled gently at me as I left.

I suppose I should call my lawyer neighbor. Someone has to represent my interests in court with the bank.

I was on the way to the Baltschug Hotel to have dinner with Vanechka. I was happy to see him. Our friendship, tested by the serious trial called "bad sex," survived honorably.

He showered me with compliments. I smiled mysteriously. "Could you kill a man?" I asked, as I set down a huge plate piled with all the salads in their buffet. I wondered why there were so few people there. There was a great selection and the price was low.

"No." He had some steamed broccoli in front of him. He had put so much seasoning on it, like fertilizer, perhaps in the hope that it would grow on the plate. Or at least, flower. "I'm too well-bred. But you, I think, are capable of almost anything."

I raised an eyebrow in mock indignation. "Are you referring to the shower in the men's locker room?"

"That too." He smiled wickedly.

I threw my napkin at him. That took care of our attitude toward that event. The tension was completely gone.

"It's my birthday tomorrow and I'm having a small cocktail party for my friends. Will you come?"

"I will, thank you." I bowed my head ceremoniously.

Vika appeared in the doorway. Spotting me, she came over with a broad smile for Vanechka.

"Are you alone?" I asked, wondering about her swimming coach.

"Not exactly," she said vaguely.

I introduced Vanechka to her. He knew how to make an impression. Vika smiled at him and made general remarks about London and British designers. She said good-bye, left, and immediately called me on the phone.

"Don't tell him it's me," Vika said. "Listen, the girls and I have taken a room, actually a suite with connecting doors. Why don't you come by?"

"What's up?" I asked.

Vika laughed. "Not what, but who. Men! The best of the best. You won't be sorry—they are gorgeous, and not a single one over twenty-two. And no blacks, don't worry."

I don't know why she thought I was a racist. "Thanks, maybe I will drop by," I said, and smiled at Vanechka. "A friend inviting me over for tea."

"Let's get some pastry here. 'It's not the rooms but the pies that make a house a home.'" He had trouble with the proverb. He must have just learned it.

"Listen, just how many proverbs do you know?"

"A whole bookful. Whenever I'm in Moscow, it's my bedtime reading. I learn the ones I like."

I didn't go to Vika's hotel room. However, I was interested in how things went. I pictured cocaine lines on a mirror brought in from the bathroom or maybe just on the coffee table, and naked tanned men dancing the cancan on the bed. Or the dance of the little swans from the ballet.

In the car I felt I was a boring and lonely drag. *And it's time for a wax job, too.*

I pressed on the gas. I was still picturing a Roman orgy from the movies. I wondered how old Vika was. *She must be over forty,* I thought with respect. *I have to tell Lena.*

It was parents' day at school. The middle-aged teacher was assigning tasks to the parents. I was offered the choice of washing windows or buying teaching materials.

At first I wanted to climb up on the windowsills, wearing a headscarf and holding rags. Bronzing in the spring sun, I would wash all the classroom windows. But after a moment's thought, I signed up for the purchase of materials. I'd send Alex.

"And now I'll tell you how your children have been doing the first three quarters."

The teacher picked up her log. I remembered that she taught the children to find the silver lining in the worst circumstances, and paid attention. "In general, not bad," she said, shutting her grade book.

"Masha must have meant the gym teacher," I thought, and decided firmly to switch my daughter to the British school next year.

I had turned the phone to vibrate before the meeting started. It stirred cozily in my pocket.

It was an unfamiliar number. The teacher was dictating a list of poems that had to be memorized over vacation.

"Hello," I said in a low voice. And wrote down "Borodino." Strange, I thought we had read that in fourth grade.

I recognized the voice of my former director. "Are you busy?" asked Boris.

"No." I wrote down "Borodino" again.

"I was asked to call you with a proposal from the company."

"I'm listening." I spoke too loudly. The teacher scowled at me over her glasses and distinctly repeated "By the sea grows a green oak . . ."

"Is this a convenient time to talk?"

I smiled with dignity at the teacher and bent over my piece of paper.

"All right." Boris, as usual, spoke very fast. "We're prepared to buy your company's brand. We feel it's better to buy a successful and advertised name than creating our own from scratch. We're offering a hundred thousand for your buttermilk."

"Three," I said, trying not to move my lips, because the teacher was watching me.

"Borodino," I wrote for the third time, and the mother sitting next to me at the double desk narrowed her eyes at me suspiciously.

"I think it would be better to discuss the details when you meet with our board. I just needed your agreement in principle." I wonder why they had Boris call me. He must have told them that he knew me and could influence me. Something like that.

I raised my hand and almost shouted, "May I be excused?"

Schoolrooms always made me feel like a little girl. With an apologetic smile, I shut the door.

Masha was playing with her friends in the schoolyard. I swooped her up and twirled around. She laughed merrily.

"Masha," I said when I caught my breath, "your Santa Claus did not lie. Everything is wonderful. We're not selling anything. We're only buying."

She hopped around on one foot, and I smiled at her, and the sun, and life. So this is what they meant by the expression, "breathing with your whole chest." Though in today's world it should probably sound like, "She was so happy, that even implant number four learned how to breathe."

The waiters
here wore
Armani outfits.
That justified
the prices
somewhat.

22.

Spring was dripping from the rooftops and the new window displays were calling for a change of wardrobe. Katya, Lena, and I, with Alex at the wheel, headed off to look at the spring-summer collections. The stores were packed.

All the popular sizes of Bluemarin at Italmoda had been bought up by late February. Lena, beseechingly gazing into the eyes of the saleswomen, begged them to bring up something from the storeroom. All the best saleswomen kept things back for "their" clients.

I grabbed a couple of colorful summer dresses and looked over at the jeans.

Katya was trying on a Valentino jacket. I didn't go to the try-on room, hoping that Katya would not like the jacket and then I would be able to get my hands on it.

"Not bad, is it?" asked Katya, twirling in front of the mirror.

"Not bad," I replied, in a rather chilly tone. But honestly.

"I'll take it," Katya decided.

Lena and I put our purchases on Katya's discount card—25 percent off, thanks to the owner of Italmoda. Katya said that if there were such a thing as a tender shark, she was one.

Then we went to Moskva. Lena was trying on her tenth pair of Chanel shoes and Katya and I studied the handbags. "We've gotten in new hair clips," the saleswoman said, "and the Cruise Collection cosmetic line. Very interesting."

Katya tried on a pair of sunglasses and turned to me. "Not bad," I said. That style didn't suit me.

"You know, his sperm have zero vitality." Katya, still wearing the sunglasses, trolled the handbag section.

"What does that mean?"

"It means he can't have children."

I gasped. Katya put a finger to her lips, and I realized that Lena did not know about this.

"What are you going to do?" I picked up a black stitched bag from the shelf, more to keep up the pretense of shopping than out of interest.

"If we don't have children, he'll leave me," Katya said bitterly, and removed the sunglasses. "Again."

"Will this go with my Dolce & Gabbana?" Lena came out in elegant polka-dotted sandals with high heels. I thought of that model as "Lagerfeld goes crazy."

"Nice." Katya smiled politely.

"To be honest, those are better." I pointed to black shoes with long laces.

"Is there any treatment?" I asked, when Lena had moved away.

"It takes your whole life." Katya sighed, and then said, "I'll take this bag." She handed it to the saleswoman, who nodded happily.

"What are you going to do?" I hurried over to the other end of the store, where I saw sandals from the summer cruise collection.

"Have a baby," Katya said when I returned.

"How?"

"Sperm bank. I've made the arrangements. He'll never know."

I nodded, pondering "never."

"Will we go look at Gucci?" Lena asked cheerfully.

"Anything but Gucci," Katya replied, and I concurred.

Having spent twelve thousand dollars, the three of us went to have lunch at Villa. I watched Katya and thought that I should be saying something important to her. But I didn't know what. This could not have been an easy decision for her. For the sake of a family. For herself. For him. I tried to put myself in his place. Which was better? To never have children or to have a child and never know that it is not yours? And what did "not yours" mean, anyway? If you bring him up and he grows up with you? If you're prepared to give up everything you have for him? Everything that you've lived for?

I wondered if I could do what Katya was doing. To understand, I would have to fall in love with someone who could not have children. I hoped that would never happen. In any case, my life's problems were just the opposite. I updated the girls about Svetlana.

"I introduced her to Serge's parents," I said with a sigh.

"What for?" Lena said in surprise.

We ordered the ravioli. The waiters here wore Armani outfits. That justified the prices somewhat.

"They're thrilled. They were left without a son, and suddenly, they have a grandson." I shrugged. "It's been a new lease on life for them."

"What about Svetlana?" Katya asked.

"She had a baby first and thought second. Basically, I feel sorry for her."

"Sorry?"

"She seems okay. She's moving in with Serge's parents."

I wasn't trying to convince them—I was trying to convince myself.

"Okay?" Lena was outraged. "In her place, would you come to the wife of your lover? Would you ask her for money?"

Lena was practically screaming.

"Never!" Katya responded for me. "She would go clean office buildings, but more likely, she would come up with something better."

I shook my head. "You don't know yet that I'm buying an apartment for her. I gave her the down payment."

"What for?" Lena looked at me as if I were crazy.

"I don't know."

"The girl has a great setup for herself. Plus Serge's parents. There's a pool in the building and a gym? And good company?" Katya asked, refusing dessert.

I ordered some pineapple.

"What if she simply fell in love? And got pregnant? And he was killed, but they had dreamed of a baby?"

I wanted to finish with: "She should have committed suicide," but I didn't.

I liked Villa. Since the waiters were in Armani, the customers should have come in torn jeans, but no one did. They all wanted to look cooler than the waiters. It never worked—the staff was always the most stylish.

I dropped by Brioni at the Radisson Slavyanskaya Hotel to pick something out for Vanechka's birthday. There were nice pajamas for twelve hundred dollars. Would a Brit be impressed by Russian extravagance? I doubted it.

"Do you have a keychain or something?" I asked, but the saleswoman did not deign to reply. She must have thought I was joking.

The newspaper stand next to the store sold wooden *matryoshkas*. I thought I had given him nesting dolls about ten years ago. "Would you have a nicely illustrated edition of Russian proverbs?"

"Unfortunately not. A lot of people ask."

A lot? I thought maybe I should publish one. But then I would hate to learn that the vendor had simply been polite.

I had some *unagi* and drank panache, a mixture of beer and Sprite. Very thirst-quenching. The Slavyanskaya has the top Japanese restaurant in town. The owner, Nobu, has one in London, too. I tried to come up with a logical connection between the two restaurants, Vanechka, and some Japanese trifle I could buy on the spot. I couldn't.

I decided to give Svetlana to Vanechka. He would find her attractive, because Serge had. I guess that meant we were the same type, although I didn't see it at all.

"Can you leave the baby with someone?" I called her as I finished my panache.

Her mother was there, her blood pressure back to normal. "Great. I'll pick you up in a half hour. Get dressed up."

I wondered why she always obeyed me. Was it because I gave her money? Because I was Serge's wife? Or because it was just me? After all, she wasn't the only one who accepted my right to command.

Vanechka had taken a small banquet room with a large balcony and bar on the sixth floor of the Baltschug Hotel. The balcony opened on a fantastic view of the Moskva River and Red Square across it, so all the guests were out there. The waiters were eager to serve strong cocktails, so no one worried about being cold.

The buffet table was along the wall. There was enough room for dancing. The guests were mostly foreigners who worked in Moscow. Many came with Russian girls.

I filled my plate lightly and went in search of the birthday boy on the balcony.

"I can't go outside," Svetlana whispered. "If I chill my breasts, I won't have milk."

Vanechka was not surprised by his present. "Is she a prostitute?" he spoke into my ear.

"No, a decent woman," I replied.

"Odd. In Moscow, people are always giving me prostitutes."

"A man's character is revealed by his presents," I quoted proudly. I had studied up the night before.

"What, what? How does it go?" Vanechka was interested in a new proverb. But I left him and Svetlana alone and stepped out onto the balcony.

I decided to celebrate my birthday here someday. But I would have more candles. And a violinist. And more black caviar. Invite a couple of television stars—it's just not decent without them, a few VIP guests (bodyguards at the door), my girlfriends, assuming they were all speaking to each other . . . I stopped. That was enough for the place to lose all its charm.

Vanechka asked if he was supposed to bring Svetlana home. "Only if it makes you happy," I replied, kissed him on the cheek, and left, without learning his plans for Svetlana.

It was a very pleasant evening. I realized why Svetlana obeyed me: otherwise I wouldn't spend time with her, considering her a rival. And I realized why I was helping her. Because I was trying to show Serge that I was better than she. For that she would not forgive me.

The next morning was cloudy. I was so accustomed to the bad weather of last winter, I did not notice right away.

The car looked as if it had been made up to look that way, for some movie with a lot of off-road driving.

My first stop would be the car wash. Moscow, as usual, was working at full blast, as if it wanted to make all the money in the world at once. There were lines at all the car washes. And traffic jams on all the roads.

By the time I reached Svetlana's, I had forgotten why I was there. Oh, yes. She was moving in with Serge's parents. I had promised to help. She had two bags of clothing, and Little Serge had five, each twice as big as hers.

She wandered around her apartment, picking up a vase or a jar of lotion.

"You won't need that," I said quickly when her gaze landed on a large clock.

The apartment looked like a hotel room when you're checking out at 6 A.M. And had gotten to bed at 4 A.M. and had not packed.

The baby slept in his crib. We had to wait for him to wake up. Svetlana was carrying things to my car. I circled the room aimlessly. I was sleepy.

"Did Vanechka bring you home last night?" I asked, when she came back up for the next load.

"Yes." She answered as if it were none of my business.

I wanted to scream at her and tell her that I had thrown him over years ago, so she shouldn't flatter herself. But I didn't.

My eyes fell on a photo album on a shelf. I couldn't stop looking at it. Serge had to be in there. Scenes from another life, unknown to me.

The door shut behind Svetlana. I put the album in my new bag and zipped it up.

They had turned Serge's room into a nursery, and they gave Svetlana the study. The cozy apartment with dark drapes was now filled with potties and colorful toys. They did not fit the interior, but that seemed very touching, somehow.

I wanted to warn my mother-in-law, but I didn't know about what. It wasn't as if she had to hide her pension from Svetlana.

In the car, my hand reached for the photo album. But I decided to wait until I got home. I wanted to look at all the photos closely and without hurrying.

Like the executioner of my feelings, I intended to examine every detail, every smile. I would enter them into my memory, my consciousness, my nightmares. That was to be my torture.

I stepped on the gas, and, on Kutuzovsky, I drove into the oncoming lane to pass traffic.

"I'm a masochist," I thought. Your heart must beat and tremble this way in expectation of pain when you open the door to the room where your husband is having sex with someone. But no woman in the world is capable of walking past that door.

There were no photos of Serge in the album. I was even disappointed. There were only four photos. A man in one of them looked familiar, but I couldn't place him.

It took several days to deal with all the issues in transferring the copyright to my brand of buttermilk. We agreed on two hundred and fifty thousand dollars, and I suspect I sold too cheaply. But I was afraid they would change their minds.

I had to hire a lawyer to handle the court case with the bank. I was determined never to take a loan that required collateral.

I had a short-term lease on the office space, so I didn't even have to break it. Everything turned out well, except for the fact that I didn't get rich.

But I hadn't started selling buttermilk to get rich. I needed distraction and to learn not to think about Serge. I had almost managed that.

Now I thought more about his driver and Svetlana's child. I had to save one and take care of the other. And then get on with my own life.

That year, spring existed separately from me. Its flowering found no resonance in my heart. It was hurtful and strange. I even wondered if that was a sign of old age. They say that it creeps up on you. The thought did not frighten me. If this was old age, I was ready to accept it, because even old age must have a silver lining, as my daughter likes to say.

For instance, you don't need to chew. Nope—everyone has false teeth now.

Your grandchildren take care of you. I have no grandchildren.

You don't have to dye your hair anymore. I don't dye my hair now.

There was nothing good about old age. I took a very bright dress from the latest Dolce & Gabbana collection from my closet. "I have to save this," I decided. "When I'm old and want a lift, I'll put it on."

I went to the party for the new line of watches at Chopard on Tretyakovsky Proezd, the most expensive block of luxury boutiques in Europe, they say.

I was supposed to meet up with Lena and Tanya. They had the invitation.

Katya was pregnant and in bed, suffering from an acute lack of estrogen. The tycoon was at her side. Her mother, too.

Lena and Tanya were late, and I stood at the door, feeling very uncomfortable.

Wearing summer sandals and practically running through the snow, an acquaintance of mine came to the store. Mariana had the invitation in one hand and the other hand was on the arm of a man who looked familiar to me.

"Don't you have an invitation?" she asked. Her man examined me frankly.

"I do," I said with a smile. "I came out for a smoke."

"I didn't know you smoked," Mariana muttered, and went through the row of bouncers.

If Lena had been another five minutes, I would have taken up smoking.

Inside, waiters offered canapés and champagne, and diamonds sparkled behind glass. I called Mariana. "Listen, who is that man with you?"

"I don't know, I met him yesterday at a gas station. I don't think he's got anything except a car. Why, did you like him?"

"Just that his face seems familiar."

Where had I seen him? At some gas station, probably.

"Really? Maybe he's some famous macho, and I'm about to get rid of him?"

"Look at the necklace Sobchak is wearing!" Lena nudged me with her elbow.

We stood at a display case and pretended to examine the new watches with emeralds. A waiter with champagne stopped next to us. Hands reached for the glasses from all sides.

"I think we can go now," Tanya determined.

She had told her husband that she had a horrible dream. He went on a hunting trip and a bear tore him apart. Tanya's husband loved hunting. She told him about the bloody body parts she saw clearly in her dream. "This portends a very, very serious illness," she said.

Tanya's husband was as much a hypochondriac as every other man. He immediately felt sick and he went straight to bed, instead of to work.

"I left," Tanya told us when we were out on the street. "That evening, I returned and told him I had gone to see a famous fortune teller. He was already green by then. The fortune-teller said that he had to have a church wedding to avoid death. He was ready to believe in whatever I told him. We're going to have a church wedding."

"You're crazy," Lena said.

"I love him. You can't understand that, girls," Tanya said, offended. "By the way, he gave me a Cartier bracelet for March Eighth. What did you get?"

"We have no one to give us presents," Lena replied for both of us. "A bear ate our admirers."

"Thought they were Tanya's husband," I quipped.

We called Katya. "Need anything? We can drop by," offered Lena.

"Thanks, the two of us are managing."

I wanted to be pregnant for a bit. To have the man who loves me smile anxiously, with gritted teeth, and bring me an apple, and a drink, and then some grapes, and then clear it all away.

"It will be warm soon," Lena said. "We could go to Turkey."

"I don't like Turkey."

"You just didn't have the right kind of vacation there."

"What are you supposed to do?" Tanya asked.

"You have to have affairs with social directors," Lena explained.

I remembered the scandal from last summer. Several girls went to Turkey for the social directors. One of them brought hers back to Moscow, rented him an apartment. Her husband found out—she blamed her girlfriend. That one blamed another one. The husbands, protecting their wives' reputations (the shame of it!), got into a big fight. And what did the girls care? Though, they probably won't be allowed to go to Turkey again.

"That's for Vika." I told them about the Baltschug.

"You didn't know?" Tanya was surprised. "They take a room every Wednesday."

We were tired of standing in the street. Even though we looked great in our festive dresses against the mounds of snow.

"Well, should we party?" Lena yawned.

"How about Gallery?" Tanya suggested.

Out of the corner of my eye I saw a camera pointed at us and had time to smile. It was a photographer from *Harper's Bazaar*. He wrote down our names for the social pages. Lena told him she was a designer.

"That's for Katya's mother," she explained.

"Do you think they'll publish our picture?" Tanya asked dreamily. "I'll show my husband to make him jealous."

Photograph . . . An association drifted up in my mind, but I couldn't quite grasp it.

We decided not to go out tonight. We didn't have a reservation at Gallery, and there was no place else to go.

I had a copy of Garland's *The Beach* in the car, and I drove home to read it.

It was so deliciously cozy to get into bed with a book: set down the tray with cookies and pieces of chocolate, turn on the light. Go back down for a Coke, because I had forgotten it in the kitchen, get back under the covers, and, without rushing, turn the first page.

I wonder if Mariana saw me inside? I thought. *She's going to think that I didn't have an invitation.*

That didn't worry me especially, but still . . . Where had I seen her date?

The sudden answer propelled me out of bed and destroyed the peace of the evening. My fingers were trembling so hard that I had trouble pushing the buttons on the phone.

"Mariana? Listen, what was the name of the man who was with you at Chopard?"

"Oh ho!" Mariana laughed. "I see he made a big impression on you. Forget him. I already have. He's just a small-time punk."

"What's his name?" I was losing patience.

"Vladimir . . . Vova," Mariana said, stunning me. "I didn't want to ask his surname. Probably something very common."

I tossed clothing from the shelves, turned purses inside out, broke a vase without noticing—I was looking for Svetlana's photo album.

There it was.

I opened to the photograph I wanted. My whole body seemed to have turned into a pair of eyes. Huge and terrified. They looked at the smiling face of a rosy-cheeked man. The mug shot did not show the piggy complexion, which is why I did not recognize him right away. "Vova," Mariana had said, and everything fell into place.

Crazed, I rushed back into the bedroom, jumped over the bed, and grabbed the phone. My mother-in-law answered. "How are things?" I asked, amazed that my voice could sound so calm.

"Little Serge is having tummy problems. He's suffering, poor thing. It must be gas. We've given him an enema and massaged his tummy."

"What's Svetlana doing?"

"She's out with a girlfriend. Grandfather and I are handling it."

I couldn't sit around waiting for her to come back. I called Vadim.

"Where are you?" My voice was close to a screech.

"What's happened?" He was very calm.

"I'll come to you. I have to show you a photo. It's Vova the Rat. Does he have a blond crew cut? Pink cheeks?"

"Sounds like him . . ."

"Tell me, where are you?"

"I'm . . ." He mumbled. "At the steam baths . . . I'll come to you."

"No. I can't wait. Give me the address!"

The baths were in Gorky-10. I put a long fur coat over my pajamas and arrived ten minutes later.

A silent guard in camouflage led me to the relaxation antechamber of the steam room. Vadim was sitting there, waiting.

"Forgive my outfit." He was wearing a long terrycloth robe.

I didn't apologize for mine. I had to take off my fur coat, it was too hot in there.

"Is that him?" I held the photo from Svetlana's album right up to his eyes.

"It's him," Vadim said with a nod.

I began bawling. Vadim was bewildered. I sat on my coat, on the floor, and howled like a whole pack of hungry wolves, only more piteously.

I'm sure Vadim had never seen me like that before.

"He looked at me . . . understand . . . Serge's killer . . . He's out partying . . . He may have wanted to pick me up . . ."

I was embarrassed. I was making a scene in front of a stranger. I was sitting in my pajamas somewhere. But I couldn't stop. It felt as if I hadn't ever cried before in my life.

I heard suppressed female squealing through the wooden door of the steam room, and a man's head popped out of the door and quickly withdrew.

"Calm down," Vadim begged. He was embarrassed. By my hysterics and by the women's cries.

The owner of the head appeared, wrapping a white robe around himself.

He'll think I'm a prostitute, I thought indifferently, covering my tear-stained face, automatically.

"Regina, dear," the man said drunkenly, taking me for Vadim's wife. "I'm just here having a steam with my sister and I asked Vadim to join us—"

Vadim stood up and pushed his protesting friend back into the steam room. "I'm sorry," he said, very seriously.

I nodded. Put on my fur coat. I wanted to cry some more. But not here.

"Shall I see you to the car?"

"No need," I whispered.

The door slammed shut behind me.

I put my hands on the steering wheel and watched my tears fall on them and form small puddles. The guard watched me dispassionately through the windshield. I turned on the radio. Very loud music. I don't know how much time passed. I didn't feel any better.

I started the car. I wasn't very proper traveling in pajamas, but you couldn't tell if I buttoned my coat.

I drove up to my in-laws' house and called them. The child had calmed down and was sleeping. Svetlana wasn't back yet. I stayed in the car, waiting for her.

Vanechka brought Svetlana back. Something ugly stirred in my breast. But I had wanted this myself.

"I hope he doesn't see her in," I thought.

Svetlana got out of the car and waved until he drove out of sight.

We entered the lobby at the same time. "Hi," Svetlana said in surprise.

The elevator doors closed behind us. "Who is this?" I showed her the photograph. I was certain he was one of her boyfriends, maybe even the father of the baby. I was ready for her evasions and lies. So I was already angry.

"My brother." She looked at me in surprise. "Why?"

"Your brother?" I thought I had only thought the word, but from the way Svetlana recoiled, I must have shouted it. "Your brother?"

I pushed her against the wall. The elevator floor shifted.

"Family of bitches!"

She pushed me away. "What's the matter with you?"

I slapped her as hard as I could in the face. My coat flew open, and for a second Svetlana looked at my pajamas, before punching me.

"What do you want from me? You're nuts!" she shouted.

I hadn't been in a fight in a long time. Maybe never. But in that elevator cabin, with its enormous wall-length mirror, I battered Svetlana and had no intention of stopping. We said no words, just furiously pulled each other's hair until the elevator door opened. Svetlana turned toward the door. I mustered all my anger into my manicured fist and punched her in the eye.

"Tell me. Tell me everything!" I gasped.

"What is there to tell?" She couldn't get her breath.

"Did they know each other?"

"Serge? Yes. They even worked together."

"Did you introduce them?"

"Yes, who else?"

"Well?"

"What else?" shouted Svetlana and burst into tears.

"What happened with work?"

"How do I know? Nothing happened. First he had a lot of money, and now he doesn't. He even bought me a mink jacket at the beginning."

I hated Svetlana because I did not believe her. From that very first minute in the restaurant. But common sense told me that she wasn't lying. She had no motive. Her brother did.

"Give me his address."

"What for?" She stepped away from me.

"Give me the address!" I shouted again.

"He's living in my apartment. Will you tell me what's going on?"

"Your son has a tummy ache. Gas. They're old people. So help them out, all right?"

We summoned the elevator because we both needed the mirror. My silk pajamas were torn, but I covered up with the coat. I tied my hair back in a ponytail.

"Tell them you fell down, and almost got run over," I said, evaluating her appearance.

Svetlana wiped the smeared mascara from her cheek.

"How's Vanechka?" I mocked.

She lifted her chin and did not respond.

I fell asleep the minute I made it to my bed. I did take off my pajamas first. But when I opened my eyes in the morning, it felt as if I hadn't slept at all.

The Rat's photograph was on the floor. "I'm going to kill him," I told myself calmly and dully.

Vadim called. "He's Svetlana's brother," I informed him.

"Her brother?" he repeated, stunned.

"Her brother. Her brother!" Tears appeared in my voice again. "You must know her, right?"

He said nothing.

"Aha!" I shouted in triumph. "You do. First you sleep with whomever, and then their disgusting relatives murder you. You are just as disgusting as your whores!"

"Do you want me to come over?"

"I do not! Go to your whore in the steam bath and check her passport. See if she's got a criminal brother or father. Or maybe she's got her own gun in her purse? Your watch is worth more than her entire life. Aren't you afraid?"

He hung up.

I threw the phone at the wall. I checked, it was still working.

Vadim called back in ten minutes. "We have to give this information to the cops. Have you learned his address? There's no guarantee that he's living at his registered address."

"And then what? We've been through this before. In court, the driver will refuse to testify. Besides the driver, they have nothing on him."

Vadim asked about his health.

"He's fine now. He walks, everything works. But he walks only inside his apartment. I can't give them a whole squad of bodyguards to accompany his family around Moscow."

"So, you don't want to tell the police?" Vadim double-checked.

"No."

I called the driver. "I found Vova the Rat," I spat out instead of a greeting.

It seemed as if he had been waiting for this call. "What do you want me to do?"

"Nothing. Just be patient a little longer."

"I'm fine. It's mother who's . . ."

"Just a little bit more," I promised.

I would take Alex's OSA pistol. It shoots through a person at ten feet.

I went down to the dining room. Alex was sitting on the couch with a magazine, as usual.

"Do you have the OSA with you?" I asked casually, looking into the teapot.

"Green tea with strawberry, just made it. I do."

I nodded. "Leave it with me. And . . . and you have the day off today."

Alex looked at me closely. "Thank you. I was going to take the car to be washed. Did you go somewhere last night?"

I muttered something and left the room. For some reason, I thought I had to be dressed all in black: black jeans, black sweater, black jacket, and black sneakers.

I told Alex I would wash the car. She watched me go anxiously.

I drove down the sunny road and I felt incredibly hurt. And I felt an enormous amount of self-pity. Everyone else was driving to work, to a date, to restaurants, to see friends. At least that's how it looked to me.

I felt every square millimeter of the gun in my pocket. Every square millimeter pressed heavily on me. At stoplights, I touched it with my hand.

I figured I needed some target practice. The beach at Nikolina Gora was the best place. In March, at any rate.

I couldn't find an empty bottle within a radius of fifty yards. I took out a canister of antifreeze from the trunk. I poured out the liquid, just to be on the safe side. I constructed a pedestal out of snow. Put the canister on it. I picked up the gun with icy fingers. Its fat belly and short barrel fit snugly in my hand.

I shot.

My arm was thrown back. The iron bullet went through the canister, throwing it far to one side, and smashed into smithereens the corner of the wooden booth where they sold tickets in the summer.

My shoulder ached. I must have dislocated it.

The test had gone well.

I got stuck on the ice for a bit and then drove out onto the Rublyovka.

I was cold-bloodedly killing Vova the Rat every second. He stood before me, looking me over as he had the night before in Chopard. Slowly I raised my arm. I had the gun in my hand. I calculated the distance and pulled the trigger. For a second, I experienced what I had done, and then once again: he stood before me. Slowly I raised my arm.

The phone rang.

I did not want to answer before I had imagined the next shot, but the ringing threw me off, so I tossed the gun on the seat and got the phone from my bag.

It was Katya. "Where are you?" she asked sadly.

"In the car."

"Are you going somewhere?"

"Babushkinskaya."

We were both silent.

"What are you up to?" I asked, trying to sound natural.

"My mother has cancer."

"What?"

Katya wept softly into the phone.

"Calm down, you can't get upset—think of the baby." I knew this was stupid. Who decided that a six-week fetus was more important than a seventy-year-old mother?

"Where is he?"

"On a business trip."

Life is more important than death. Friends are more important than enemies.

He wouldn't get away from me, that Vova the Rat. He was doomed. He was doomed the second he decided to kill my husband over some stupid shares. She said that her brother had no money. That meant the business deal was a failure. And Serge was dead. Bastards like Vova should meet the wives first.

I went to see Katya. Katya's mother was dying. The only way Katya could help her was to bring painkillers to the hospital. But that was the problem. It could be given only by prescription and only in amounts that were clearly not enough. No amount of money could help.

"I can't believe that."

Katya looked at me helplessly. "I can't do anything. It's madness."

"At triple the price?"

"Not even at ten times the price."

I felt fear.

"Do you know what she said? Just a week before she learned . . . she had cancer?"

"What?"

"In life, like in a bad book, only the beginning and ending are important."

Under other circumstances, I might have been put off by the maudlin phrase.

Katya burst into tears. "Her ending is horrible. You weren't there. You didn't see . . . And there's nothing I can do, do you understand? I could buy the entire floor of the hospital, the entire hospital, all the doctors and aides for a year, for ten years! Understand? But I can't make it so it doesn't hurt."

I counted out some drops of valerian tincture into water for Katya and then drank it myself. "None for me," Katya said. "I've had two bottles in the last few days."

"How's the pregnancy going?"

"Hormonal deficiency. But I don't have a stomachache any more. That's a good sign."

She cried some more. "But she does . . . Maybe at this very moment, she's in pain."

I went home when Katya went to bed. It was four in the morning.

I fell asleep in the bathroom, right on the pink tile floor, rolled up into a ball.

I woke up three hours later. I wanted to pray.

I thought about how I had to get up, take the gun, go to Babushkin-skaya, and shoot the Rat. That thought was deep in my brain, it was all around me, filling all available space like a concentrated substance that barred me from the rest of the world. It was like a wall, and I was banging my head against it.

I was nauseated, and I had aches in my stomach, head, hands, and legs. And in my kidneys, liver, and spleen. My heart did not beat, it was scraped. By a sharp rake.

I begged God to return Serge to me. Even with Svetlana. With the baby. With twins, triplets, with a gay lover, with—it didn't matter. As long as he existed. And sometimes, maybe just once a year, he would give me one day of his life—say on March 8th, and I would spend that day with him tight in my arms, and I wouldn't let go. I would breathe in his scent. And I would die—once a year—of happiness.

I pulled some clothes from the shelves and dressed. If anyone had asked what I was wearing, I couldn't have answered.

I took the OSA from the seat and put it in my bag.

I drove out of the yard and turned on the windshield wipers. Then I turned them off. Tears filled my eyes. I wiped them away with my hands, drove, then wiped some more.

I wanted to be a little girl. I wanted my mommy. God, I didn't want to be driving anywhere. I was so tired. This nightmare had to end.

I stopped for red lights without noticing. I passed cars without bothering to look in the mirrors.

I shed bitter tears and pedestrians looked at me curiously. I looked back, in case there was a red-cheeked man with a blond crew cut among them. Then this torture could end faster.

I turned into Svetlana's yard in a state close to madness. There was an ambulance and two police vans at the lobby door.

I went upstairs, unable to believe what I was guessing.

There were people in the apartment, primarily in uniforms or white coats. In the spot where Masha's crib—rather, Little Serge's crib—had stood was a white chalk outline of a human body in a strange position. Not far from it, blobs of tomato paste, like the ketchup ads. It was blood, of course.

"Who's been killed?" I asked everyone, and they all turned to me.

They asked for my ID. "Who's dead?" I persisted.

"According to his driver's license, Vladimir Molchanin. Who are you to him?"

"His wife." I began weeping. They gave me water.

I sobbed and hiccupped. But I was beginning to feel better.

I did not care how I looked. I was hysterical. I understood that, but I couldn't stop.

A woman in uniform and a horrible dye job tried to calm me down. She patted my back and I wept in her arms. "Everything will be all right," she said wearily. "Time heals, believe me. Everything will be fine."

I listened and gradually calmed down.

"Do you have somewhere to go?" she asked.

I nodded.

"Then go. We'll call you in later, all right? In a few days."

"All right," I agreed, obediently.

My cell phone rang. "Answer," she suggested. "You shouldn't be alone now."

"Hello." My voice was dull and dead.

It was Vadim.

"Where are you?" he asked tensely.

"Babushkinskaya."

I nodded to the uniformed woman and went out with the phone.

"What the hell are you doing there?" he shouted at me, probably for the first time in his life.

"Did anyone see you?" he asked in a moment, in his normal tone.

"Yes. Everyone," I replied in a capricious tone. No one had been this upset on my behalf in a long time, and I was goading him on.

"Let's have lunch. We need to talk."

I agreed. In two hours at Veranda.

We had tuna and salmon tartare. Then I ordered beef stroganoff with mashed potatoes. For dessert I had Napoleon torte baked either by the mother or the housekeeper of one of the owners.

"Who killed him?" I asked Vadim.

He shrugged. "A killer." He might have been answering "How much is two times two?"

I looked at him, but said nothing. Obviously, he would tell me nothing. Fine.

"I didn't imagine you could be there so early in the morning."

"I told them I was his wife."

His eyebrows shot up in amazement.

"I don't know, it just happened," I said with a smile.

"They'll be looking for you. I'll take care of things, of course, but I need time."

"Oh, God, not again!" I almost choked on my mashed potatoes.

"You'd better leave town. For a month or two."

"That's awful," I said, because I had seen this scene in the movies. "You have twenty-four hours to get out of town."

Personally, I didn't feel awful at all.

I called the bodyguard agency while Vadim was talking to some friend.

"You can stop guarding them," I announced cheerfully.

"They found him?"

I muttered something vague and hung up.

"Do you have money?" Vadim asked.

"Yes."

"Call Dudina. Today's Friday, you have to leave no later than Monday."

Dudina took care of holidays for everyone on Rublyovka. "Are you sure, Vadim?" I whined.

He smiled gently. "If you get very bored, call me—I'll fly over to amuse you."

Dudina said that she couldn't organize a visa over the weekend, and without a visa I could only fly to the islands. Or Turkey. I thought of the Turkish social directors and refused.

"What about Monday? Can you take care of a visa that morning?"

"To Europe, no. My dear, it's simply impossible. Give me three days."

"Dudina, I have to leave on Monday. Somewhere warm and in a first-class seat."

"Those are your only conditions? Nothing else?"

I shrugged. "That's all."

"Then you will. Start packing. I'll call you this evening and tell you where you're going."

Vadim looked at his watch and made his excuses. "I'm late."

I decided to stay on. I would order a glass of red wine and think things through.

Vadim and I kissed good-bye, avoiding each other's eyes. I wanted to say something nice to him, if only a simple "thank you," but he did not give me the chance. He turned quickly and left without a wave.

I called the driver. I told him he didn't need a bodyguard anymore. He wanted to ask, but my dry tone made it clear that I wasn't going to go into detail on the phone. I thanked him sincerely and apologized for all the problems we had caused him.

I had already asked for the bill when I saw Lena arm-in-arm with Oleg through the glass front door. "I hope we're not rivals?" Lena whispered in my ear.

"Only if you're a candidate for Miss Moscow 2006," I replied, and Lena burst out laughing.

Oleg walked me to the car. "I've fallen in love with your friend," he announced.

I managed a smile. "Don't worry," he said, looking me straight in the eye, "I won't tell her anything about you."

I nodded. He probably expected the same from me, but I said nothing.

I wondered where they had met.

The driver's brother called. He said he wanted to talk and would come to the office on Monday. "What about?" I asked politely.

"Well, you know . . ."

"I don't understand."

"Our mother, she . . ."

"I'm leaving the country on Monday. A woman named Alex will deliver money to you. All the best."

"I'm leaving the country," I told Alex. "For a long time."

"Take me with you." She gave me a pleading look.

"I'll think about it," I promised. She clicked her heels stupidly and smiled.

"I'm leaving." I realized that the idea made me happy.

We had a big send-off. Everyone was there except for pregnant Katya. Her mother's health was getting worse. She was dying.

Tanya invited everyone to her wedding in Jerusalem, at a Russian Orthodox church, of course.

Kira did not bring her dog, because Blondie had developed dandruff from all the dye jobs, and you couldn't hold her in your arms. Her husband never did return. Kira dreamed of the moment when he would show up at her house again.

"I'll punch him in the nose," Kira promised, "and then I'll knee him in the groin."

Lena was happy with her affair with Oleg. Chopard hearts sparkled on her ears—his gift to mark the anniversary of their first week together.

Veronika had finally accepted her husband as he was and stopped being upset by his frequent disappearances. She stopped threatening him with divorce or the police. He stopped hitting her.

We were drinking champagne in Green on Kutuzovsky. There was no more expensive restaurant in Moscow, with a clientele to match. I had a gold discount card, for twenty-five percent.

"Does anyone have a congressman in the Duma?" Veronika asked, too drunk to pronounce the words clearly. "We need a law on student driving from the age of sixteen with a licensed driver in the car."

"Why?" Tanya asked.

"Igor is giving his daughter a car for her sixteenth, and she doesn't have a license."

"Hey, who's that with Olya?" Lena changed the subject, darting her eyes toward the owner of a sports store who went in for a lot of plastic surgery.

The last operation had left her breasts shifted to the side so much that they kept her arms from hanging along her sides naturally. She looked a little like a small weight lifter before an event.

Olya was with the husband of one of our acquaintances. "He's not her husband," Tanya corrected. "They didn't get married."

"What's the difference?" Kira insisted. "They have a baby. Girls, let's not say hello to her."

We started a lively conversation so that when Olya passed by our table, we were too busy to notice her. Only Tanya gave her a surreptitious smile and nod.

At nine we started to leave. My flight was in two hours, to India.

. . .when a nice young man in a turban carrying a folding chair behind me will not be an annoyance.

23.

"I found a fantastic place for you," Dudina told me Friday night. "First class, Boeing plane, only six hours' flight, excellent weather—moderately hot, excellent hotel, with a spa, and not expensive."

I listened with bated breath.

"India," Dudina revealed. "I'll have the visa for you Monday morning. Bon voyage."

I had a fear of flying, so Lena gave me a tranquilizer especially for that. "You're not supposed to mix it with alcohol," she said in passing. "It has an effect on the memory. You end up repeating yourself. But you're planning to sleep, right?"

Lena tugged at my sleeve, as I headed for the VIP lounge. They were already boarding my flight.

"No one reserved VIP for you." Lena was having trouble speaking and kept looking over at the duty-free liquor shop. We decided we had time for a quick drink at the bar. Then another one.

By the time I got to the gate, they were paging me.

First class was full. My neighbor in the seat next to me ordered a cognac before takeoff.

I looked out the window at the flickering lights of the runway, as everything to do with Moscow grew distant and unimportant.

When we could unfasten our seat belts, I reclined my seat.

"Would you like a cognac?" my seatmate offered. I thought for a second, and brought my seat back up.

We drank cognac and chatted pleasantly. I told him everything I read about India over the weekend.

The stewardess woke me as we were getting ready to land. "Good morning," I said to my seatmate, trying not to breathe on him.

He nodded and smiled. "I can't wait to see India," he said.

"Yes. You know, they have a very interesting custom." I was about to tell him that women wear a bracelet for every year of marriage.

"I know." He stopped me gently. "I heard that story seven times yesterday."

Fortunately, the stewardess interrupted us then.

We got out of the plane. The air in India is filled with spices and adventure. The Delhi airport looked like Moscow's Sheremetyevo Airport in 1988. Even in 1990. Several taxis proudly proclaimed air conditioning. I chose one of those.

"Have you changed your itinerary?" my fellow traveler asked politely. His name was Kostya, but I didn't remember that. We were staying at the same hotel and had made plans to travel there together. A chauffer-driven Mercedes was waiting for him.

I didn't see any other Mercedes on the road to the hotel.

But I did see an elephant striding along the sidewalk with a man in snowy white clothing; a pack of monkeys on a leash (an idea for Kira to replace Blondie); an absolutely naked man strolling along in a bored manner; a huge number of beggars in ironed trousers and colorful saris embroidered with spangles. In Moscow I could wear one to a party. There were also cows, lean and self-important, lying in the middle of the road and acting as if the cars were not in their way.

The streets were cleaner than Moscow many times over, which was a pleasant surprise. Of course, Kostya did explain that central Delhi was quite different from the outskirts. He promised to take me on an excursion.

The Oberoi Hotel was not in midtown—it was a resort hotel. I unpacked and thought about what I would do here. I decided on a tour of the city.

I traveled in taxis that looked like our old Volgas, and I felt like a colonial wife. The Indians treated me respectfully, as a white woman, and with the exotic locale, every day was an adventure.

Occasionally I called Moscow. There was a new restaurant called Shatush, and that was the place to be. I didn't miss anyone, except my mother and daughter.

Kostya kept going off to Jaipur and Bombay. He exported Russian cars—Zhigulis—to India. One day, when he came back, he invited me to dinner. "There will be two Indian princesses. But the dress code is casual. How's your English?" he asked merrily.

I didn't go to dinner with the princesses. I imagined how we would become friends: they would introduce me to their circle, we would start going out to restaurants, going into town, having parties, and celebrating birthdays. In other words, doing everything I did in Moscow. I was frightened. I had come for solitude and a very different life.

"Don't come if you don't want to," Kostya said. "But you're wrong to think that it's so easy to become a girlfriend of Indian princesses."

I smiled meaningfully.

There are many poor people in India. But the Indians like comfort. That's why every poor man has an even poorer man who serves him.

Once I found myself on a long street where nails were sold. Only nails. Lots of them. This was typical of India. There seems to be a lot of everything. People, elephants, flowers, everything. And nails. Next to one of the stalls, an elderly Indian man, dressed only in light, wide trousers, was shaving. He looked very poor. His stall looked poor, as did his wash-faded trousers, his dirty feet, his exhausted face, his rusty straight-edge razor, and the cracked mirror he was using. Another Indian was holding the mirror for him. His trousers were even more faded, and his face even more exhausted. At a respectful distance from that pair stood yet another man, holding a bowl of water. It would be hard to imagine someone more impoverished than he. Except for the fourth man, who held the brush. He passed it to the one with the bowl, who would nod haughtily. Then he would dip the brush in water and hand it to the mirror holder with a servile smile. The mirror holder did not deign to give his assistant as much as a smile. He looked beseechingly at the man who was shaving. The whole process ended with a cripple who held the towel. The relative whiteness of the towel underscored the blackness of his face. It was burned and covered with pustules. I looked behind him, not knowing what to expect. But I saw only a puppy, lazily lolling in a mud puddle.

I was sorry that I didn't have a camera with me. And I was glad that I hadn't been born the daughter of a nail vendor in Delhi. I tried to imagine coming out of the stall and telling this fresh-shaven papa that he looked wonderful. And he tells me to wash the bowl. And I nod to the young Indian woman behind me. In a pallid sari. Even though I must say that I never saw one in a pallid sari. Even the lowest beggar woman would pass the dress code in any Moscow club.

If I were to compare India to America, Delhi is Washington. The luxurious and happening place is Bombay. Like New York.

In Delhi life flowed steadily, the morning sun turning to noon heat and then evening cool. I came to love Indian cuisine, learned three words: *aga* (good), *handji* (yes), and *nandji* (no), and started each day with a trip to the hotel spa.

Ayurvedic massage with four hands on a large slab of wood with a hollow carved out for the human body ended with drops of hot coconut oil on the forehead. After the massage, your old and weary body seemed to stay in that wooden depression while your soul, as pure as an infant's, but with hands, legs, and belly, rose from the table. You looked at them as if you had never seen them before. The two helpful masseurs in waist cloths brushed out your hair, washed off the oil, and saw you out, bowing and saying words that seemed miraculous but probably translated as, "thank you, come again."

I also loved scalp massage with hot oil. At the very first second you think it's burning you, but then a pleasant relaxation spreads throughout your body and it really seems that the masseur's careful fingers are moving bad energy and everything bad along your hair, from the scalp to the ends, where it falls off, dissolving without a trace in space. That is the ayurvedic teaching.

Kostya took me to Agra. A majestic and gorgeous place. We dined in an ancient palace, with the tables right on the lawn, and I copied the movements of the folk dancers. They surrounded me and I moved my hands smoothly, eyes narrowed, hips swaying in rhythm to the music, and it felt as if I had never had any other life.

"In a past life I must have been a dancer," I told Kostya as I approached our table, dancing.

"A dance hall girl," Kostya said.

"Not at all." I put on a bit of indignation. "On the contrary, an Isadora Duncan."

"No. She died young."

"Then Charlie Chaplin. That's it. I was Charlie Chaplin."

I did his famous walk down the lawn.

"A man?" Kostya asked suspiciously.

I laughed. "You were a woman then."

"Me? I doubt it."

"Are you a misogynist?"

"Even if I had been one, everything would change now. But, truly, I never hated women."

I smiled coyly.

Kostya smoked a cigar and looked at me the way every woman needs to be looked at to achieve her highest fulfillment—when she feels that she is the most beautiful and most desirable woman in the world.

That was how I felt.

When Kostya spoke, he always gestured. I liked that he had handsome hands and long, slender fingers. I found myself copying his gestures, without meaning to.

He always had a glimmer of a smile when he spoke. Even about the most serious things. A boyish grin.

I also liked that he knew how to live in the here and now, a rare talent. When he was with me, he was with me. Nothing else mattered. And so it seemed that nothing else existed. And I felt like the most important person in the universe.

Kostya bought me a red sari, and we spent several hours figuring out how to wrap me in it. We learned that red saris are worn as wedding dresses. "You're not married, are you?" I asked him with feigned horror. "I could be misunderstood in this outfit."

Kostya assured me that he was absolutely free and went to find out what the groom is supposed to wear. The vendors smiled into their thick mustaches and were mystifyingly silent. That was quite intriguing.

In Agra, I began collecting decorative pillowcases: embroidered and beaded and mirrored, quilted from various decorative fabrics, appliquéd with animal designs. I spent three days on the collection. When I reached one hundred twelve pillow cases, I smoothly segued to collecting necklaces of semiprecious stones.

Life there was so sunny and measured that it filled my soul with a peace I had not felt in ages. I thought that in this strange, almost fairy-tale city, I was protected from shock and catastrophe. I wanted every day to be like yesterday, and yesterday like tomorrow. I wanted to know that nothing would ever happen in my life again. I was ready to have the biggest problem in my life be the selection of a new sari. The bright silk saris cost five dollars, and I could buy one every day.

I began seriously considering moving here forever. My old dream of a big white house with southern breezes and a tanned youth in a turban who would respectfully carry my folding chair behind me could come to pass in Delhi. I actually thought that having a chair dragged around behind me all the time would become annoying, but the rest was exactly what I wanted.

I decided to familiarize myself with the real estate situation in Delhi. That would not obligate me in any way. I just wanted to know what was for sale and how much it cost. Not to buy, but to know that the possibility existed. Or maybe buy? And feel myself a bit adventurer and a bit conquistador? As Gumilev put it in one of his poems, "I start out and walk cheerfully, resting in joyous gardens and leaning over abysses." What if this really was what I had always wanted? Not the abysses, but the rest in gardens?

I went to a few agencies and they showed me various sweet houses. But not the house of my dreams. Yet.

I was buying the cream of my collection, a bright necklace, when Vanechka called. He told me that Serge was not the father of Svetlana's baby. I set the beads down on the counter and walked out of the little store. The sun hurt my eyes and burnt my shoulders.

"What did you say?" I asked, realizing that I was not surprised in the least. It was as if I had always known.

"The baby's father abandoned her. Svetlana's girlfriend told me." Vanechka coughed guiltily into the phone. "We're having an affair. I may even marry her."

A beggar hopped over to me. He had one leg and one arm. I turned away.

"Marry whom?"

"Svetlana's friend. But that's not for sure yet."

I stayed on the line, waiting for some folk wisdom, but it did not come.

I went into the shop and bought the necklace, bargaining desperately from four dollars down to one.

What a bitch that Svetlana is, I thought, lying in the pool in the shade of palm trees. I felt badly for Serge. And I felt great satisfaction knowing that my husband had only one child, Masha.

I thought about the apartment in Krylatskoe and about Serge's parents. I wanted to be in Moscow and to hit Svetlana on the head with something very heavy. But then I imagined what it would be like for them to lose Little Serge. They couldn't bear another loss. I would not permit that.

I called. My mother-in-law picked up. After a detailed story about the child's successes in waving his arms and legs, she told me that Svetlana had gone away. "She said she couldn't explain completely, but it was on some expedition," my mother-in-law said, without regret. "Will you be back soon?"

"I don't know," I said, and it was the truth. "Maybe you can come here with Little Serge."

I didn't have dinner with Kostya that evening, I didn't swim in the pool at night, and I went to bed early. Kostya sent flowers and a book in Russian, quite rare there, to my room. Garland, *The Tesseract*. The line, "a cockroach ran across the floor like a miniature skateboard," made me laugh and I fell asleep, forgetting Svetlana and Moscow once more.

In the morning I decided that I wanted to collect ancient musical instruments. Like everything else, there was an abundance here. I planned to hang them on the walls of my Indian house, which would be found for me someday.

Kostya supported my initiative, and while I was having breakfast he brought me a huge, dilapidated drum, that took up exactly half my room. I decided to keep it in his hotel room. I also offered him part of my pillow collection, but he refused. I didn't offer the necklaces.

I went to the old city with Kostya, where he had some business to do. We met an old wrinkled man named Shiam. He was hammering out a sphere from a hunk of marble, and inside the sphere there would be dozens of tiny but just as perfectly shaped spheres, reflecting all the colors of the rainbow. The work would take five years.

Shiam was seventy-three. He was not sure that he would complete it before dying. So every day students came to him. And every day he sent them packing.

"What is the sphere for?" I asked Kostya. He translated my question into Hindi.

"It's beautiful," replied Shiam, and looked into my eyes.

I smiled with understanding.

"He wants to know if you'd like to learn." Kostya translated his staccato, sibilant phrases.

"Me?" I was nonplussed.

"He says you will be able to do it."

I pictured myself for the next five years sitting in the hot sun monotonously hammering away at the marble.

"Thank you for the trust, of course." I looked over at Kostya and saw that he had no intention of rescuing me, he was enjoying the situation too much.

Shiam offered me the instrument, which looked like a tire iron. I didn't want to hurt the old man, so I took the iron.

"All right, all right, let's go," Kostya laughed and said something in Hindi. "Otherwise, what if you like it? What will I do with the sphere? My room is full of your drums as it is."

Shiam smiled at us with his excellent white teeth, which all Indians seem to have regardless of age.

"His feelings weren't hurt?" I asked anxiously.

"No. I told him that you couldn't do it because you were pregnant."

"But I'm not pregnant." I was embarrassed for some reason.

"Well, you will be," Kostya promised, without looking at me.

I like men who speak in declarative sentences. Without beseeching question marks.

I did not argue with Kostya. I turned away to hide my smile.

The next day I had a call from the realtors. I drove up to my dream house, making my way through a thick layer of pedestrians and pedicabs.

I recognized it right away. By the peace and satisfaction I felt in the huge sunny living room with French doors that opened into the well-tended garden. I picked out rooms for Masha and my mother. Mother would definitely like the spacious bedroom with sliding glass doors leading to a terrace, and Masha . . .

I walked around the house yet again, and I could hear the voices of my family inside and I could picture how we would breakfast on this veranda and have parties for our neighbors in this garden.

I told the agent that I was ready to look at the paperwork. Kostya had promised to help me with that.

I thought about how my life had held happiness and joy. And love. And friends. And dreams that came true and hopes that had been justified. And I was grateful to fate for giving it all to me.

How fortunate I was to have my daughter and my mother. I would devote my life to them. I would bring up Masha, and she would grow up to be better than I, and more beautiful, and kinder. I would move Mother into this house, and she would not have to worry about taking care of herself ever again. She would grow exotic flowers and plants.

I strode through the colorful streets of Delhi and I was happy.

Kostya had flown off to Goa for a few days, so the house deal had to wait.

I decided to call home once the house was bought and furnished. I decided to buy it on a bank loan and pay it back once I sold my house in Moscow. If I wanted to go to Moscow, I would stay at the Baltschug. But I was certain that I wouldn't want to go.

I thought about the house every waking second.

During lunch at the Taj Hotel I realized that I needed a guest room. I thought about which room it would be and the furnishings for it through dessert. First I wanted to make it an ancient Russian *terem*, the rooms for the palace women, but then settled on my favorite Pop Art of the 1980s.

Bright collages with Marilyn Monroe on the walls would go very well with the Indian style of the rest of the house. It would add a certain charm.

I went through ideas for Masha's room. Everything had to be beautiful and festive. Mother's bedroom would be refined and the bedspread would be trimmed in gold lace.

I found a whole street of furniture stores. They stunned me. I had never seen furniture like that. Huge ancient benches and trunks, heavy tables and dressers of teak. With brass fittings and delicate carving. The spirit of the ages was palpable in them.

I examined the unusual objects, hypnotized. I went from store to store and could not believe that I could own them.

Suddenly, I pictured the black hammered trunk in the living room of my Moscow house. And the ancient mortar in the entryway. You could put an umbrella in it.

This furniture would cause a stir in Moscow. I could open a gallery. There was no need to spend money on renovating it—these objects would be astonishing in an absolutely ordinary interior.

I asked, "Could you show me the wholesale prices?"

I didn't want a house in Delhi anymore. I didn't want peace and quiet anymore. I realized that my paradise was something else.

I would open a store in Moscow. Beautiful and unusual. People would come and admire things. They probably would not buy at first. Only the most fashionable and progressive ones would buy my furniture. Then it would become fashionable for all. But I would be first.

The heat in Delhi suddenly seemed too hot and the sun too bright. For the first time I thought of Moscow with nostalgia. Alex would meet me at the airport. I pictured her happy face.

But first I would call her and instruct her to find a space for the gallery. Somewhere in the center of town. With a good entry. About four hundred square meters of space.

I wondered how Veronika was doing. And Katya. And what that new restaurant, Shatush, was like.

The salesman's dark eyes found mine. "Hi. These are the wholesale prices," he said in English.

I smiled with all my heart. *We'll be friends,* I assured him mentally. "But you'll have to change your prices. Lower them."

I think he understood, and smiled back warmly.

After all, I thought, *I can buy a house here in a few years. At a time when a nice young man in a turban carrying a folding chair behind me will not be an annoyance.*

24.

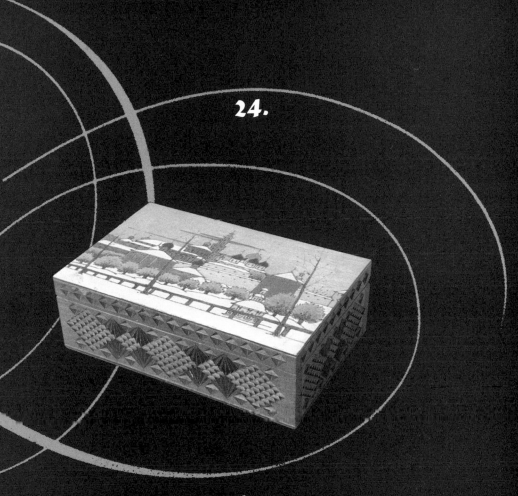

Kostya agreed to finance this project.

And all the other projects in my life.